D0386924

I CONQUER BRITAIN

I
CONQUER
BRITAIN

DYAN SHELDON

CANDLEWICK PRESS
CAMBRIDGE, MASSACHUSETTS

Copyright © 2006 by Dyan Sheldon

First U.S. edition 2007

Library of Congress Cataloging-in-Publication Data is available.

Library of Congress Catalog Card Number pending

ISBN 978-0-7636-3300-4

2 4 6 8 10 9 7 5 3 1

Printed in the United States of America

This book was typeset in Sabon.

Candlewick Press
2067 Massachusetts Avenue
Cambridge, MA 02140

visit us at www.candlewick.com

Contents

You Never Can Tell 1

I Come Up with a Lot of Really Good Reasons
Why I Should Have Thought of Swapping Lives
with Some Poor Fool Years Ago 6

My First Encounters with the Natives Aren't All
Bad, but They Aren't All Good, Either 17

Day One and Already I'm Wondering if
Normality Is Everything It's Cracked Up
to Be 35

The Pepto-Bismol Experience 42

A Nice Cup of Tea 56

Had I Crossed the Ocean or Fallen Down a
Rabbit Hole? 66

I Meet the Czar Who Escaped the
Revolution 74

And Then There Was the Queen Who Could
Have Started a Revolution 84

Seeing the Sights and Stuff Like That 93

So This Is How the Normal People Live 107

I Take a Walk 114

With Friends Like These 125

Things Change Suddenly, the Way Things
Do 140

I Have One of Those Days 151

This Is the Kind of Thing That Happens When
You Don't Stick to the Tour Bus 159

The Perfect End to a Perfect Day 173

If There's One Thing You Can Always Depend
on, It's the English Weather 183

The Final Episode, in Which We Bid a Fond
Farewell to the People and Places of Putney 197

... And Say Hello Again to Good Old
Brooklyn 199

You Never Can Tell

TO EXCHANGE: ONE SLIGHTLY USED LIFE IN BROOKLYN, NY. INCLUDES INSANE FAMILY, ESCAPEE SACRIFICIAL ROOSTER, DESTRUCTO PIG, AND INCONTINENT CAT. WILL CONSIDER ALL SERIOUS OFFERS UNLESS YOU LIVE IN A WAR ZONE OR SOMEPLACE REALLY COLD.

That's the ad I would have put in the paper if I'd thought of it, but I didn't think of it. Even though I spent a lot of time dreaming of being in a different place or with a different family (somewhere more interesting than Seventh Avenue with people who don't make normal seem like some unachievable goal), it never ever occurred to me to swap my life with someone else. I mean, you wouldn't, would you? Who would want it? (If *you* don't want it, why should anyone else?) I never thought of going to Europe, either. I knew Europe was out there, over the ocean, but I'd never thought about going there any more than I thought about visiting the North Pole (which is obviously not something I would consider for *one minute*). Not until Mr. Magoo (otherwise known as Mr. Apolony, our principal) announced that the school was sponsoring a trip that summer. I was pretty much in sleep mode by the time he said it, but as soon as he did, my mind woke up and my soul leaped with the joy of destiny seen. A summer in Europe! Why hadn't I thought of that before? I didn't just *want* to be on the trip—I *had* to be on it. All of a sudden, I could practically hear the narrow, cobbled streets of the Old World calling plaintively. *Come! Come!* they cried. *Cherokee Salamanca, we've been waiting hundreds of years for you! We can wait no more!*

None of my friends were interested.

Angelina said she didn't "get" Europe. Angelina said that as far as she was concerned, Europe was just a bunch of old buildings. (To be fair to Angelina, you can't really expect her to get totally warped out by the idea of intercontinental travel. Her ancestors were murdered, lied to, enslaved, and cheated by Europeans. Whereas my ancestors were mostly the ones doing the murdering, lying, enslaving, and cheating.)

Bachman didn't "get" Europe either. He couldn't see why I wanted to traipse around a pile of old ruins.

Bachman's my best friend, but let's face it: he can be a real pain in the butt when he wants to be.

2

And this time he *really* wanted to be a major annoyance.

I said that Europe isn't old ruins; it's a treasury of great architecture and art.

Bachman made a face like he'd just swallowed a beetle. "You mean all the great architecture and art that wasn't bombed into oblivion or stolen in some war, right?"

I said that was the stuff I meant.

Bachman said if he wanted to see old paintings, he could go to a museum, which he wasn't likely to do since he doesn't like museums. (To tell you the truth, I'm not really a museum kind of person, either. They're sort of like zoos for paintings. I always feel sorry for the pictures, stuck in a room with all these other paintings they don't know and all these people trooping past them who are probably thinking about lunch or what they're going to buy in the gift shop.)

"Europe isn't exactly a museum, you know," I informed him. "It's a real place. People have lived there for millions of years."

"People've lived in caves for millions of years, too," said Bachman.

"Well, maybe you missed this, Robert, but most of our ancestors came from Europe."

"Not mine," said Angelina. "Mine came from Colombia."

"Only some of them," I said. "The rest all came from Spain. Which I'm pretty sure is part of Europe."

"Well, mine totally came from Europe," said the ever-helpful Robert Bachman Jr. "And the reason they came here was because they were either starving or going to be killed if they stayed." He smirked. "So why would I want to go there?"

Well, obviously he wouldn't.

And I couldn't go because my mother, Jake, is economically challenged. (She could be the poster child for the Working Poor.)

"Who's going to look after Gallup and Tampa if you're in Europe?" asked Jake. (And I could be the poster child for Slave Labor.) "And anyway, we can't afford it."

Beginning, middle, and end of story.

Or so I thought.

But then Jake came home from work on her birthday with the news that she'd made a deal to send me to Europe.

I said, "Who with? The devil?"

She said with Caroline Pitt-Turnbull. Caroline Pitt-Turnbull is her friend from when she went to art school in London. Caroline has a daughter my age, and this daughter, Sophie, was desperate to get out of London for the summer and she'd jumped at the chance to come to Brooklyn (she was obviously also clinically insane).

I said, "But England's not *in* Europe."

Jake said that it's *in* the European Union, which she figured was pretty much the same thing. "And it's a lot closer to the continent than Brooklyn is."

This was true, but so is Greenland.

"Except London's not Paris, Athens, or Rome, is it?" I figured London was pretty much like New York, only they don't have yellow cabs and the accents are different. "Maybe it has queens and princes and stuff like that, but that doesn't exactly make it the ancient cradle of civilization or anything."

"Oh, for God's sake, Cherokee." Jake made one of her what-have-I-done-to-deserve-this faces. "Do you want me to call Caroline back and tell her it's off, and you can stay here and spend the summer keeping your brother and sister from destroying the neighborhood?"

Well, if she was going to put it like that. I mean, I wanted someplace really old and stuffed with the ghosts of history and time, but I wasn't above compromise. Let's face it, there wasn't really much of a choice between sweating and eating pizza in Brooklyn and riding double-decker buses (possibly with guys who look like Orlando Bloom) and drinking tea from china cups in London. So although I was disappointed, it wasn't exactly like being impaled on the horns of a dilemma (as my grandmother, who knows about a trillion hokey old sayings and never gets tired of repeating them, would say).

"No, that's OK," I said. "I'll go to London."

(Lesson for Today: Take what you can get, or you may not get anything.)

I Come Up with a Lot of Really Good Reasons Why I Should Have Thought of Swapping Lives with Some Poor Fool Years Ago

I'm a very adaptable kind of person (because, with my family, you have to be), so I got over my disappointment at not seeing Paris, Rome, Madrid, and places like that pretty quickly. I Googled "London, England" and discovered that it has just as much history and old buildings and stuff as they do anyway. It also has tons of ghosts and pagans dancing naked in the moonlight. We might have the occasional voodoo ceremony in Prospect Park (which is how we got our rooster, who is a runaway ritual sacrifice), but you're not likely to run into any naked Wiccans in Brooklyn—that's for sure. Since I like to keep in constant touch with the Earth Goddess, I found this all really interesting. More than interesting. It suddenly seemed pretty obvious to me that (even though I hadn't known it) England had always been part of my destiny!

And Mr. Young in the grocery store said that even though they might have a few ghosts and pagans hanging around, the English are still the most civilized people in the world. "They've got the best accents," he informed me. Then Mr. Young did his impression of an English accent for me. "Jolly good, old bean . . . I say, what a good show . . . Toodle pip . . . What a rotter . . ." That pretty much exhausted what he'd learned from old movies. "And the best tailors and the best gardens," he went on. "Don't forget, Cherokee, England was the birthplace of the Industrial Revolution."

I knew it has the best tea and that it's the birthplace of the Beatles, the miniskirt, and the punks, but not those other things.

"I'd like to know where we'd all be without the Industrial Revolution," said Mr. Young. "That's what I'd like to know."

According to my gran, Sky, we'd all be a lot better off if we still had to make our own clothes and bread (the Industrial Revolution is just one of the *millions* of things she holds against the civilized English), but I didn't say that to Mr. Young. I didn't want to burst his bubble.

Bachman, however, wanted to burst every bubble I had.

"What about me?" asked Bachman.

I said, "What about you?"

"You know." He looked down at his feet. "I thought we—I thought we were going to hang out this summer."

What he thought was that we were going to start going out officially. We were always on the brink.

7

I acted like I didn't know what he was talking about. "But this is my big chance. You can hang out with Sophie while I'm away. She'll need someone who's sane."

You'd think there was an entire miniature solar system on the toes of his boots, he was staring at them so hard. "Yeah, right. And who are you going to be hanging out with?"

He meant boys, of course (he's about as subtle as a nuclear bomb). He was afraid I was going to fall in love with Orlando Bloom (or someone who really looked like him) and never come back. I kept acting like I didn't know what he was talking about. "Well, how do I know? I'm not a mind reader. I'll hang out with whoever I meet."

"Yeah, right."

I wanted to punch him. "Will you please stop saying 'Yeah, right,' like that? It *is* right. I've never met any English people before. I don't know what to expect."

But Bachman did.

He finally tore his eyes from his boots. "You mean you don't know that the English are all snobs and the guys are all gay?"

"Oh, really? Does that mean they reproduce through mitosis?"

Now he was looking like he wanted to punch *me*. "OK, so maybe they're not *all* gay. But they're definitely into cross-dressing."

I asked if he meant like that man in Texas whose wife divorced him because he liked to wear her old

8

cheerleader's outfit, and Bachman said that you can't count Texas.

By the time departure day dawned, I figured that the only downside to going to England was that I hadn't done it sooner. I could think of about a zillion reasons why I should have.

The first fifty or so were my family.

As an example of the kind of thing I have to put up with on a daily basis, we didn't have even one teeny, tiny suitcase that was suitable for intercontinental travel. I know for a fact that all other families have at least one, and most have a whole set that matches and has working locks and stuff like that. I had to trawl around the attic for something to put all my stuff in, and all I came up with was Grandpa Gene's old army duffel bag. I dyed it black and painted silver bats and stars all over it but there was no way anybody was going to think I bought it at Gucci or that it was part of a set.

What also happens in all other families is that everybody you don't actually live with calls you up days before you leave to wish you a safe journey and give you whatever good advice they've got (you know: don't drink the water, don't sit on the toilet seats . . . stuff like that). In my family, they all called up about an hour before I was supposed to leave for the airport—and good advice was about as abundant as water in the desert.

"Don't forget, honey," said Grandpa Gene, "if

any of those Limeys give you a hard time over there, you just remind them that we won the war for them."

"Don't you forget that through your veins runs the blood of Irish martyrs," warned my gran. "You can't trust the English. They're heartless, bigoted oppressors. Everything they did to the Indians they did to the Irish, the Scots, and the Welsh first. If you're smart, you'll keep your eye on the door and your back to the wall."

Even my dad called (collect, of course). Sal said if there was one thing I needed to know about the British it's that they call erasers "rubbers."

Most other families have regular pets like a dog or a hamster. We have Houdini, the runaway rooster, Pancho Villa, the cat with a really bad attitude, and Bart (otherwise known as Destructo Pig). Living up to his name *and* his reputation, Bart ate the backpack I was going to use as carry-on. I found what was left of it under the kitchen table approximately five minutes before we should have left for JFK.

I couldn't find anything to use instead, so I had to run to Mr. Young's store and get a cardboard box that used to have cans of peaches in it. Then I had to get dressed. Jake said I should wear jeans and sneakers and put my hair up so I looked normal. "You don't want to bring attention to yourself and end up spending hours getting through security," said Jake. But I figured this was *my* adventure and I wanted to look like me, not someone else. So I wore my black lace skirt, the black top with the diamanté stars all over it, my black lace tights and my twenty-hole black boots. I put on six star earrings (three dangling and three studs) and all my bangles. It took me twenty minutes just to get my eye makeup right. Everybody was already outside, waiting for me impatiently (tapping their feet and looking at their watches) by the time I was finally ready.

Another thing normal families have is a regular car that can go over thirty without something falling off so it doesn't take them half a day to get to the airport, but we have a VW van that remembers Woodstock. You can live in it, but it's worth your life to try and ride in it.

The next two reasons why I figured I should've swapped my life eons before were Bachman and his dog, Bruce Lee. They went with us to see me off. Bachman was in one of his dark, surly, argumentative moods.

"Mark my words," he said as he threw my duffel into the back of the van. "You're going to wish you'd changed your mind. The English are all wusses. You'd have a lot more fun if you stayed here and went camping with me."

"Yeah, sure." I mean, what girl would want to go to London, one of the most exciting, cosmopolitan cities in the world, when she could be trekking through the Catskills with a fifty-pound pack on her back and a bear alert out? I passed him the cardboard box. "In your dreams."

11

The entire Scutari family was on their front porch across the street, waiting to give me the official Brooklyn send-off.

"Yo, Cherokee!" Mr. Scutari winked. "You look like a refugee with that duffel and that box. Only you're going the wrong way!"

Mrs. Scutari and her daughter, Barbee, came down to the van. Mrs. Scutari had a box of Oreos, and Barbee had her baby.

Mrs. Scutari shoved the cookies into my hands. "Just in case they don't have nothing to eat." Somebody told Mrs. Scutari that the English eat cucumber sandwiches (which she says is the same as bread and water), and ever since, she's been convinced that the only reason the British colonized the world was to get a decent meal.

"It's going to be great," Barbee assured me. (And this from someone who probably can't find Brooklyn on a map, let alone England!)

I said I was counting on it.

"I mean, at least they speak English, right?" said Barbee. "Instead of something else like in those other countries."

Mr. Scutari and his sons stayed on the porch. The Scutari men all dress exactly the same—T-shirts, jeans, and baseball caps that say SCUTARI & SONS— and they all look pretty much the same, too (like they're the last people you'd want to see come through the door if you ran one of those all-you-can-eat buffets). Since it was more or less the cocktail hour, they were sipping cans of beer.

"Cheerio, Cherokee!" George Scutari raised his can. "Have a good time."

"Thanks."

"That goes for me, too," said Errol. "Don't drink too much tea."

"I'll try not to."

"Did I tell you what my uncle told me?" asked Mr. Scutari.

"Yes." Mr. Scutari's uncle was in England during World War II. "Yes, you did."

Mr. Scutari told me again. "The only thing the English have is rain. No chocolate, no oranges, no nothin'. They didn't even have toilets in the house when my uncle was there. You had to go outside. No heat neither. But it never stopped raining. That's why they've all got arthritis and such bad teeth."

"Don't you listen to him." Mrs. Scutari patted my arm. "They've got the Queen." Mrs. Scutari has gone on record as saying that she doesn't care what people say about the Queen being stuck up and everything because she wears that lovely tiara all the time. Mrs. Scutari is a fan.

"I know." I'd also heard Mrs. Scutari's opinion of the Queen before. "She's had all the problems anybody has."

"That's right," said Mrs. Scutari. "Maybe more. What with that husband of hers and her boys and those grandsons, and poor Princess Diana, may she rest in peace."

Jake honked the horn. "Let's go, Cherokee! You

won't get to London before Charles is king if we don't get a move on."

"Don't forget to take a picture of that big clock they've got for me!" called Mr. Scutari as the van rumbled into the road. "I really like that clock."

I sat up front to navigate. My mom can get lost just going around the block. Bruce Lee sat on my lap.

Bachman leaned over my shoulder, talking, but I wasn't totally listening. I was thinking about England. Crumpets and cricket . . . bowler hats and double-decker buses . . . Mary Poppins and Sherlock Holmes . . . the Beatles dressed in miniskirts . . .

In my mind, I was just sitting down to my first cup of real English tea in a real cup (as opposed to an old, chipped mug with a broken handle) when Bruce Lee brought me back to the moment by throwing up all over my lap.

"You see?" said Bachman. "He misses you already."

What Jake missed was the road to JFK.

"Goddamn," Jake muttered as LaGuardia appeared over the horizon. "How did we wind up here?" She took her eyes off the road for a second to glare at *me*. "I thought you were supposed to be navigating."

I said I didn't think I could be held responsible for Bruce Lee's digestive problems. (Lesson for Today: *Never* take your eye off the map, even if it's covered in dog barf.)

By the time we finally found the John Fitzgerald Kennedy International Airport there was no time for long good-byes.

They all walked me to the entrance to International Departures.

Gallup gave me a picture he painted of the whole family (including Bart, Pancho Villa, and Houdini) on the front porch. He wanted to know if I was going to come back with an English accent.

"Toodle pip, old bean," I said. "You never can tell."

Tampa gave me a wooden box to keep my hair clips and earrings in. She had decorated it with glitter, beads, and pictures from magazines. She wanted me to say hello to Harry Potter for her.

"Righty-ho," I said. "If I run into him, I'll be sure to give him your warmest regards."

"Just try not to bring disgrace on the family," said Jake.

As if.

I asked Bachman if there was anything he wanted me to bring him back from across the rolling sea.

"Just you," said Bachman.

"That's like that Bob Dylan song!" shrieked Jake, and she started singing.

I took that as my cue to leave.

I looked back before I stepped inside.

Jake was still singing. I could see the Christmas tree earrings Tampa gave her for her birthday (they were really cheap) swinging from her ears. Tampa

15

(all in yellow because it was a yellow day) was standing on one leg in the tree pose. Gallup, wearing his YOU ARE WHAT YOU EAT T-shirt with the photograph of a footless factory hen on the front, was sitting on the floor beside Bruce Lee. Bachman, looking like a squatter, threw me the peace sign.

They all waved (including Bruce Lee), and Tampa shouted "Bonny voyage!" loud enough to be heard back on Herkimer Street.

I gave them a big smile and waved back.

I was pretty sure I wasn't going to miss them.

My First Encounters with the Natives Aren't All Bad, but They Aren't All Good, Either

I wasn't really what you'd call a seasoned flier. I was used to traveling by land. Not that I was scared or anything like that (I mean, have you *seen* the statistics for road accidents?). I just figured air travel would be even less interesting than waiting for a dial-up Internet connection (which on a scale of one to ten is about minus three million). You know, nothing to look at but clouds, nothing to do but watch some dumb movie or try to sleep all squashed up with your knees touching your chin. There wouldn't even be any of the distractions you get when you travel by trailer (like a couple of llamas in the road or a woman and a wolf pup hitching a ride—the kind of thing that used to happen all the time when we traveled with my dad). So I was pretty much resigned to a long, boring flight while every cell in my body positively *vibrated* with excitement (which meant *hours* of really slow torture). But like Sky always says, everything has a price—and the airbus was the price I had to pay to get across the Atlantic before I had to be back in school. I figured it wasn't really a bad deal.

I sat next to Mrs. Anne Beeker. Unlike me, Mrs. Beeker was what you'd call a seriously unhappy flier. She was terrified of being more than a foot off the ground. Mrs. Beeker was from a place called Kent that she pretty much wished she'd never left. She told me at least a hundred times that this was only her second plane ride before I even got the peaches box into the overhead locker. She was the only person who actually watched the flight attendants when they demonstrated how to blow up your life vest and where the light and the whistle were and stuff like that.

"Aren't you afraid you won't know what to do if something happens?" asked Mrs. Beeker.

I said I figured we'd be dead before we hit the water anyway, so it didn't matter, but she didn't laugh like I thought she would.

Before we took off, Mrs. Beeker couldn't stop talking about how scared she was, but once we were actually in the air she just sat there staring out her window like she wanted to be the first to know if the wing fell off.

I read the in-flight magazine (which wasn't exactly going to cause William Shakespeare to roll around in his grave) until it was time to eat.

That's when the first disaster happened. Jake forgot to book me a vegetarian meal. I swore up and down that we'd ordered it and confirmed it and everything, but it didn't do me any good because they didn't have any more. Joe, the head flight attendant, was really nice about it. He ran around trying to get me extra portions of salad and cheese and crackers.

That didn't do me any good either, though, because before he came back with them, Mrs. Beeker was sick all over me. She was really, really sorry. I said it didn't exactly matter because Bruce Lee had already barfed on me in the van.

After Joe tried to clean us off with those little towel things, I tried to get some sleep, but just as I was nodding off, some guy fell down drunk in the aisle next to me. There was a big hullabaloo about that. By the time Joe got him back to his seat, Mrs. Beeker had recovered enough from being sick to let terror take her over again. I spent the rest of the flight telling her all about my family and why I was going to London and how Bart ate my backpack and stuff like that to take her mind off things like falling into the Atlantic like a really big rock.

I was beginning to think that we took a wrong turn somewhere and were never going to get to London when the captain finally said, "We're about to begin our descent toward Heathrow, ladies and gentlemen. I'm afraid it's a typical summer day in London—rain and more rain."

"Oh, my God, we're there!" I couldn't help it— I just screamed out loud. I had to lift myself up to look out the window next to Mrs. Beeker. Rain!

Just like Mr. Scutari said. I couldn't have been happier if the Queen had been down on the landing field waving her tiara at me.

Mrs. Beeker disentangled a couple of my earrings from her hair. "Thank God, you mean." She said that with real feeling.

I patted her arm. "Don't you worry, Anne, we're almost there." And then I remembered something I'd learned from English shows I'd seen on PBS. "As soon as you get home and have a nice cup of tea, you'll forget all about this." Have a nice cup of tea! I was practically a Limey already.

Mrs. Beeker patted me back. "And you'll want to get something to eat, love. You must be famished."

I said it was OK because the food wasn't really worth eating (even if you could keep it down), and anyway I'd had Mrs. Scutari's Oreos to keep me alive.

Mrs. Beeker was still weak from being so scared and sick and everything, so even though I wanted to get off the plane as fast as I could, I had to hang around to help her get her stuff from the overhead compartment.

It was like hours before I finally got to the door.

Joe shook my hand. He said I was a real trooper and wished me a brilliant holiday.

I made a mental note to remember that the English say *holiday* for vacation and *brilliant* for great. I figured I was a natural at intercontinental travel.

The woman who checked my passport was named

Araya Sparrow. She said *Cherokee Salamanca* was almost as unusual as her name, and I said I'd rather have hers because hers sounded kind of magical while mine sounded like something that had just crawled out from under a rock. Araya was really interested to find out that I'd never really been out of the States before unless you counted Mexico, which I didn't.

"Now fancy that. You must be well excited." She hoped I had a good time.

"I am well excited," I told her. "And I'm going to have a brilliant holiday." I hadn't even left the airport and already I was speaking another language. I figured there had to be some English blood mixed in with the Irish martyrs.

I got to where our bags were being unloaded just in time to see my duffel moving away from where I was standing. There were so many people all huddled around the carousel that there was no way I could push through them to grab it. But I didn't want to wait for it to come back around. I was in a hurry. So I dumped my box on the floor and sort of launched myself at the carousel. You couldn't say I landed gracefully, but it was still a pretty good dive (if I do say so myself). I scrambled over a couple of suitcases that were in my way and grabbed the strap of the duffel. Unfortunately, it didn't really solve my problem since my bag was still going around on the conveyor belt—only now I was going around with it.

I was trying to figure out how to get off in a

dignified way (you know, without actually knocking anyone over or my skirt riding up to my chin or anything like that) when someone grabbed me with one hand and my duffel with the other and hauled us to the ground.

This was Kev. Kev was a big guy with really short hair; he was wearing a Nike hoodie, warm-up pants, and a Las Vegas T-shirt and had a gold hoop in one ear. For a second I almost thought I was back in New York, but then he spoke.

"That was some leap." He was definitely not American, even if he wasn't wearing a dress and didn't sound anything like Mr. Young when he put on an English accent. "Do you do kung fu, or are you a gymnast?"

I told him I do yoga. "It keeps me flexible."

Kev got me a "trolley" and threw my duffel aboard. Kev said I was going to love London. He said it had some great street life and all these really interesting markets and graveyards and stuff like that. "Trust me," he said. "I can tell you're going to take to it like a duck to water. It's a cert. It's a dead cool town."

I repeated all my new words over in my head as I steamed toward customs. *Holiday . . . brilliant . . . trolley . . . cert . . . dead cool . . . holiday . . . brilliant . . . trolley . . . cert . . . dead cool . . .* I couldn't wait to get out of the airport. I picked up speed.

From the expression on the face of the customs inspector, I figured his job was a grim and unhappy one, and that his life outside of Terminal Three probably wasn't much better. He waved me over with a flick of his fingers as soon as I stepped through the doorway.

"You don't mind if I take a look in your bags, do you?"

I did mind. My destiny was waiting for me. I said that to tell him the truth I was kind of in a hurry.

He nodded. "I noticed that."

I said that if it was all the same to him I'd just as soon skip it this time because not only my destiny but the Pitt-Turnbulls were waiting for me.

He nodded again. "We'll start with the box of peaches, shall we?"

I tried to reason with him. I said I took the green lane because I didn't have anything to declare.

"Look at me!" I cried. "Do I look like I'm smuggling drugs or guns or stuff like that?"

He said I'd be amazed what he'd seen in his hundreds of years of going through other people's belongings. He said he reckoned that anything was possible.

I said I'd be willing to swear on the Bible that he could trust me. But reason never works with most adults I've tried it on, and it didn't work with him.

He waved at my cart. "We'll just have a little look to make certain."

Nothing ever goes the way it's supposed to with my family. When you live with people like that, you learn to take disaster pretty much in your stride.

23

It's why I'm so adaptable. "OK," I sighed, "but I really hate to see you wasting your valuable time." I heaved the box onto the counter.

"I've only ever been searched once before," I told him as he started to untie the string around the box as if he was defusing a bomb. "When we drove into Mexico by mistake. My mother has no sense of direction."

"Is that so?" He took out the presents from Gallup and Tampa.

"She's totally hopeless. She can't even find Brooklyn without a map, and we've lived there for six years."

He looked at Gallup's painting for a few seconds. Then he opened Tampa's box.

"Anyway," I went on, "even though we were only in Mexico for like ten minutes, they tore the whole van apart."

He moved on to my CD player and CDs. "And did they find anything?" he asked without looking up.

"Of course not. We hadn't been there long enough to buy a taco."

Next he took my makeup and toiletry bag and the books I'd brought along for all those quiet English afternoons sitting in the garden sipping tea.

"It was all pretty traumatic. They kept asking us how long we'd been in Mexico and Jake kept saying five minutes."

Next came my jewelry bag and the candles and charms I use for my altar to the Earth Goddess.

"I believe in keeping my spiritual self in touch with the cosmos," I explained. "You can't live just on bread, can you?"

The inspector said, "Ummm." Then he reached in and took out the woven bag Sal brought me back from Thailand.

"You'd don't have to look in there—"

He pulled out a strip of rag and held it up. It looked pretty grubby hanging from his hand like that. "And this is?" There were long, dark hairs wound around it.

It wasn't like I hadn't tried to warn him. "That's for my hair. You know, to make it wavy?"

He dropped the rag back in the bag. "In this country we have curlers."

He finally came to the black velvet bag covered with stars that Sky gave me for Christmas. "And what have we here?"

"That's my herbs and oils and stuff like that."

The oils were in tiny blue bottles, and I'd put the herbs in old film canisters.

He opened one of the bottles and sniffed. "I think you'd better come with me."

He took me into this windowless room with fluorescent lights like in some cop show. The only furniture was a big Formica table and a couple of plastic chairs. It was about as cheerful as a morgue. I figured I was lucky I was in the most civilized country in the world or I might really be in trouble.

He took everything out of my duffel (including the stuff I hadn't exactly had time to wash before

I left and my yoga mat) and spread it all out on the table. The whole time he was doing that, he was asking me every dumb question he could think of.

Where was I going?

(Well, where did he think I was going, Katmandu? Um, duh . . . Don't tell me I got off at the wrong stop?)

I said London.

Where had I come from?

(A night of passion between my parents sixteen years ago near the Cherokee Reservation—I'm lucky they weren't near a Ford plant.)

I said New York.

Who packed my bag?

(The upstairs maid—couldn't he tell I was way too busy having my summer designer wardrobe fitted to do it myself?)

I said that in my family, if you wanted something done, you did it yourself.

Was my bag with me the whole time?

(No, it went to the airport by itself.)

I said of course not—they put it in the cargo hold with everybody else's luggage.

It went on like that for about a hundred and fifty years. I was just about to walk out and find a toilet when the door opened and another customs guy came in.

He smiled at me. "I'm Mr. Wottle." He didn't smile at the inspector. "What's going on here?"

The inspector told him what was going on.

Mr. Wottle looked at all my stuff and then he

looked at me and then he looked at the inspector again. "Have you gone mad? She's just a girl."

The inspector said that they have soldiers in Africa who are only eight years old.

"Not wearing lace skirts they don't," said Mr. Wottle.

The inspector held up my velvet bag. "She's got some suspicious substances in here."

I said I didn't. I said what I had was essential oils and the herbs I use when I'm making spells. "Change can be stressful," I explained. "I figured I might need some help from the Earth Goddess."

Mr. Wottle had a sigh a lot like my mother's. "I'll take it from here," he said to the inspector. He nodded toward the door. "You go back to your station."

Mr. Wottle was a lot more user-friendly than the inspector. I told him all about how I'd come to London because I was swapping lives with Sophie Pitt-Turnbull, just like in a reality TV show.

"Her parents are Robert and Caroline," I said. "He's a writer and she's a painter. Just like my parents." Which was just about all I knew about them except that Caroline used to drink Pimms and lemonade and like ABBA and Robert doesn't write travel books (which is what Sal writes) but novels.

Mr. Wottle was worried that the Pitt-Turnbulls might have thought I'd missed my flight and given up and gone home.

"I'll go with you, see you're all right," he said as

he helped me repack my stuff. "If they're not there, I'll put you in a cab myself."

To tell you the truth, I'd been a little bummed out by the inspector and all his questions and his sniffing and him giving me the evil eye and everything. I'd started to think that maybe I should've stayed in Brooklyn after all if this was the kind of reception I was going to get. But Mr. Wottle restored my good spirits. Except for the accent (which also wasn't anything like Mr. Young's) and the fact that he was bald as a pool ball, Mr. Wottle reminded me of Grandpa Gene. I was sure that everything was going to be totally Boom Shiva from then on.

Living up to the reputation the English have for being gentlemen, Mr. Wottle insisted on pushing my cart.

"She was a lot like you when she was your age, our Gem," Mr. Wottle was saying as we stepped into the arrival area. "The hair and the clothes and the makeup and all. Had to go all the way into London to get her a pair of Goth boots for her birthday one year. Sprained her ankle twice the first week."

That's when I spotted the Pitt-Turnbulls standing behind the barricade. They didn't look like a writer and an artist (not any writer or artist I'd ever lived with). He was wearing slacks and a jacket (a jacket in July—I figured that was what Mr. Young meant by civilized), and she was wearing this flowery dress and a string of pearls. They looked like they were going to a wedding (which is the only time either of my 'rents would ever get that dressed up). If Caroline hadn't been holding a sign that said CHERRY SALAMANCA on it in really neat lettering, you would have thought that they'd wound up at the airport by mistake. This wasn't really what I was expecting. What I was expecting was a couple pretty much like Jake and Sal (only English of course, not so financially challenged, and together). But I could tell right away that the Pitt-Turnbulls weren't *anything* like the Salamancas. They looked so straight and totally normal that they could have stepped out of a fifties sitcom (you know, where nobody ever shouts or argues or has a really bad day). I wasn't discouraged by this, though. First of all, I figure that everyone has hidden depths. You think you know what a person's like by looking at them, but you don't. You just know what they look like. A person can look like a bum but have the heart and soul of a saint. And a person can look like the most respectable person in the world and be a total lying crook. Second of all, I decided that this normal thing was really a bonus, since I was used to abnormal.

Caroline was smiling but it wasn't what you'd call a happy smile. It was the kind of smile you make when you realize you're on the wrong bus. You know, like you have no idea where you're going but you know you're going to be really late for something earthshakingly important and that something really cosmically awful is going to happen but you hope that if you keep smiling, it won't be as bad as you think.

Robert's smile was more like his pants were too tight.

I decided that the only thing to do was convince them really fast that even though I probably wasn't anything like their daughter, they weren't going to regret taking me into the bosom of their family. I waved. "Yo!" I shouted. "Here I am!"

Caroline saw my hand moving back and forth. Her smile pretty much went into rigor mortis. And her elbow went into Robert's ribs. He looked over and totally stopped smiling. Caroline's fingers fluttered in my direction.

You had to feel sorry for them. I mean, we were pretty much in the same boat, really. They were expecting somebody like their daughter (which meant they were doomed to incredible disappointment). And also they didn't look really adaptable.

"You won't believe what happened!" I cried cheerfully as Mr. Wottle and I reached the Pitt-Turnbulls. I went to hug Caroline, but she was pretty fast for someone who dressed up to go to the airport, and she dodged out of my way. She kissed the air on each side of my head instead. I figured this must be some English thing and kissed the air on each side of her head. It seemed to work.

Caroline welcomed me to London. "Robert." She touched his arm. "Robert, this is Cherry."

Like he couldn't figure that out for himself.

Robert nodded. "Well . . . well . . ."

The way he was looking at me, you'd think he hadn't known whether he was expecting a Masai warrior or a teenage girl.

"We were beginning to get worried about you." Caroline's mouth was still smiling, but her voice was wringing its hands. "Weren't we, darling?" Darling nodded. Caroline turned to Mr. Wottle. "She hasn't been arrested, has she?"

Mr. Wottle and I both laughed, but you could tell that Caroline wasn't trying to dazzle us with her incredible sense of humor.

"Oh, no, no," Mr. Wottle assured her, "nothing like that. We've just got to be a bit thorough these days . . . You know, terrorists and all."

Robert was staring at my eye makeup so hard that I figured my mascara must've run or something. "Well, you certainly know how to make an entrance," he said to me.

"I am sorry if there's been some bother . . ." Caroline managed to look at me and Mr. Wottle at the same time, which made it hard to tell which of us she was apologizing to.

"No bother." Mr. Wottle touched my shoulder. "It's just that the young lady has an intriguing assortment of potions with her. Made the inspector a trifle nervous."

"It's incredible!" I laughed again. "They thought I was smuggling drugs! Can you believe it? Me! I don't even take prescription medicines."

31

Robert was nodding as though this came as no surprise to him. "Did they, now?"

"Oh, how dreadful for you," murmured Caroline. "You poor thing."

I didn't want her to think me and England had gotten off on the wrong foot or anything. "Oh, it wasn't dreadful. It was great, wasn't it, Mr. Wottle? I haven't laughed so much since the time Gallup put Houdini in Big El's car."

Caroline was the most determined smiler I'd ever met. "Houdini?"

"Houdini is Gallup's rooster," I explained. "And Big El's our landlord."

"Of course," muttered Robert.

"We had a good laugh, right enough," said Mr. Wottle.

I said I couldn't wait to tell Jake and Bachman.

"Jake?" Caroline blinked. "Bachman?"

"Jake, you know, my mom? Your friend?"

"Oh, Jacqueline!" Caroline made a sound that was somewhere between a laugh and a sneeze. "I didn't realize . . ." Her smile fluttered. "Sophie calls me Mum."

"A rose by any other name," I said. "And Bachman, he's my best friend. He's promised to keep an eye on Soph while she's in Brookyln. You know, make sure she doesn't die of mega-boredom or anything."

Caroline didn't really look like this was the best news she'd ever heard, but she kept on smiling. "Why, how kind of him."

"So, are these your bags?" I could tell from his voice that Robert was a man who believed in regular suitcases, probably matching. "The big one looks like it's been in a war."

I said that it had. "It was in Vietnam with Grandpa Gene. He still won't use chopsticks because of what happened to him."

"Well, then . . ." Robert looked at Mr. Wottle. "Perhaps we'd best be getting on. Let you get back to work."

After Mr. Wottle said his good-byes, Caroline turned back to me and said she was sorry about the rain. "I was so hoping it would be nice for your arrival."

I'd never had anyone apologize to me about the weather before. "That's OK. We have rain in Brooklyn."

"Well, that's all right, then," said Robert. "We wouldn't want Sophie to get too homesick over there across the pond."

It was kind of exciting speaking the same language and not understanding what they were saying. "The pond?"

"You know. That body of water you flew over."

"You mean the Atlantic Ocean?"

Robert didn't laugh—he chuckled, which is not a sound you hear very often in Brooklyn. "You Americans. Whoppers instead of burgers . . . Latte Grande instead of a large coffee with milk . . . You do love to exaggerate."

Caroline patted my arm really lightly, like it

might be hot. "Let's get you home and I'll make you a nice cup of tea."

Now that was more like it. Right then I figured that a nice cup of tea was probably what had been missing in my life for the past sixteen years. "Cool. We don't really have tea in Brooklyn."

"That's what you get for dumping the last lot we sent you in the harbor," said Robert.

He grabbed hold of the cart. "I've got to pay for the parking. I'll take the lift and meet you at the car."

I thought he meant he had to get a ride to the car, which is something that Jake's always having to do. "You're just like my mother. She always parks so far away that we might as well've walked in the first place."

Robert gave Caroline a look. "What did I say? Separated by a common language."

"He means he's taking the elevator," Caroline explained.

Lift, not elevator . . . Lift . . . lift . . . lift . . .

"Boy," I said, "I'm going to have to start taking notes with all these new words. All I knew before I left Brooklyn was that you call erasers *rubbers*."

Caroline's smile flickered. "And what do you call them?"

"Erasers."

"No, I meant what do you call rubbers?"

"Condoms."

Day One and Already
I'm Wondering if Normality
Is Everything It's
Cracked Up to Be

I probably don't need to say that the Pitt-Turnbulls' car wasn't nearly forty years old and four different colors, including rust. It was a late model black BMW, and it was so clean it looked like it'd just rolled out of the showroom.

"Wow!" I said. "A real car."

There was nothing on the floor, no junk piled up in the back, no duct tape holding parts of it together. I was almost afraid to sit down in it, in case I got it dirty or accidentally scratched the upholstery or something. Caroline gave me a thin smile as I climbed into the back. She was afraid for me to sit down, too.

We weren't there more than a couple of minutes when Caroline started worrying that something had happened to Robert.

"I wonder what's keeping Robert." She gazed across the parking lot like we'd already been on the road for hours and she was looking for a rest room. "I hope he hasn't forgotten what level we're on."

I said he didn't seem to me like a person who'd forget where he put the car—that's the kind of thing my mom does.

Caroline smiled at me in the rearview mirror. "That's what worries me. Perhaps something's happened to him."

I really didn't think there was that much to get worked up about. I mean, what could have happened to him? It wasn't like he had to cross the Amazon on a raft (or Flatbush Avenue on foot)—you know, anything you might consider dangerous—to get back to the car.

Caroline said he might have been mugged.

I pointed out that there were about a million people coming and going.

Caroline said that he might not have the right change for the machine.

I said, "You mean it doesn't take bills?"

Caroline sighed.

I started looking around for signs of England while Caroline went through every possible disaster that could have happened to Robert, but parking lots aren't one of the things that change from place to place. You know, they all look like a set in a cop movie (like someone's going to start shooting at you in about three seconds). So except that the cars all had their steering wheels on the wrong side there weren't any signs of England. I could still have been in New York.

Caroline had just decided that Robert might have had a heart attack while waiting for his turn at the machine when he finally turned up. He'd gone back to get a paper.

If it was Jake, she'd have made him really sorry he kept her waiting like that, but Caroline just smiled. "We were starting to get worried that something had happened." She turned her smile on the paper. "You know, you could have bought that at home."

"What? And go back out again?" Robert got into the driver's seat. "I've been up since the bloody crack of dawn, Caroline. Once I get into the house, that's where I'm staying."

Now that I was actually in the bosom of the Pitt-Turnbull family (well, in their car), I started feeling a little weird. Like a dolphin who suddenly finds herself on the backseat of a BMW.

And I was also starting to feel really bad for Caroline and Robert. I figured that if I was feeling weird, they must be feeling even weirder. They were the ones who were taking the dolphin home for tea.

Not that they let it show or anything. Angelina's mother was right about the English being so polite. Robert was all fasten your seat belt and no one minds if I put on the radio, do they? And Caroline kept apologizing for the weather and how long it took us to actually get out of the parking lot.

We drove to Putney with the window open because Robert said he liked a bit of fresh air when he drove. (I was pretty sure that wasn't true. I mean, if he wanted fresh air, he'd pretty much have to drive on a different planet, but I didn't say anything. This was obviously just more politeness. I didn't think he really wanted a good whiff of pollution and a lap full of rain; I thought he just didn't want to choke to death on the smell of vomit coming from my skirt.) Robert concentrated on driving, and Caroline concentrated on smiling at me in the rearview mirror. It made me really nervous. I was starting to think that maybe she had some horrible genetic defect that made it impossible for her not to smile. Like if you told Caroline some really, really bad news—that the world was about to be hit by an asteroid the size of Saturn, for instance—she'd keep right on smiling, even if there were tears in her eyes. I bet she had to stay away from funerals.

That's why I started talking. Jake always says that one of the biggest mistakes she ever made was teaching me to speak. She says that when I was little, I fell asleep talking and woke up in the middle of a sentence. But even by my standards, I talked a lot all the way from the airport. I couldn't shut up. It was because I was all off center. As soon as Caroline (politely) asked me how my flight was, I was off. Blah blah blah blah . . . I couldn't find a suitcase. . . . Blah blah blah blah . . . Bart ate my backpack. . . . Blah blah blah blah . . . Bruce Lee threw up on me in the van. . . . Blah blah blah blah . . . Jake got lost and went to the wrong airport. . . .

Blah blah blah blah . . . Mrs. Beeker thought we were all going to die. . . . Blah blah blah blah . . .

"So then, Mrs. Beeker threw up all over me, too." I laughed so Caroline would know I thought it was funny and she didn't have to apologize. The apologizing wasn't relaxing me any more than the smiling was. "It's like I'm being stalked by vomit."

It didn't work.

"Oh, you poor thing. I am sorry," said Caroline.

"So there was a big commotion about that, but Joe — the flight attendant — Joe was a total angel. Mrs. Beeker was really embarrassed, but I told her that you could tell from how fast Joe mopped everything up that he'd done it before. I said she wasn't the first person to lose her lunch on a plane and there was no way she was going to be the last, and that made her feel a lot better."

"Oh, dear . . ." murmured Caroline.

"But that wasn't the end of it." I could see Caroline's smile kind of flinch in the mirror, but I couldn't stop myself. "Then this dude fell down drunk right next to my seat."

Caroline said she was sorry.

"No, it was cool. It was better than watching the dumb movie," I went on. "And anyway, after all that drama, I didn't even mind about my meal."

I could see Caroline straighten up in her seat. "Your meal?"

"Did I forget about that part? They ran out of vegetarian."

Caroline looked around. "Pardon?"

"Vegetarian," I repeated. "Probably Jake forgot to order it—you know what she's like—but I didn't tell them that. I pretended they'd made a mega-mistake." I shrugged. "Not that it did any good, but you've got to try, don't you?"

Caroline was still looking at me as if I'd suddenly started talking in Spanish.

"Vegetarian? Are you saying you're a vegetarian?"

Well, what did I expect? Trust Jake to forget to mention anything that might be important. "Don't tell me she didn't tell *you,* either!"

"No, I'm afraid not." Caroline's smile was getting a little grim. "But I'm sure she had a lot on her mind." She blinked a few times, probably wondering what she was going to do with the half a cow she'd planned for supper. "What about fish? Do you eat fish? Or chicken?"

I'd always thought the word *vegetarian* was pretty self-explanatory, but it looked like it was open to interpretation in England.

"No," I said, "just vegetables."

"Perhaps we'd better stop at the supermarket." Caroline touched Robert's arm. "Darling, do you think we could go by way of Waitrose?"

Robert glanced over like he'd forgotten we were in the car with him. "What?"

Caroline asked him again if we could go by way of Waitrose.

"Oh, Caroline . . . now? You know I'm expecting an important call from my agent. I'd really like to go straight home. Besides, I thought you did the shopping yesterday."

"I did, darling, but that was before I knew that Cherry doesn't eat meat."

"Doesn't she?" He passed the turn-off Caroline was pointing to. "I don't see the problem," said Robert. "Let her eat cheese."

The Pepto-Bismol Experience

By the time we got off the highway (otherwise known as the motorway, which if you ask me makes it sound like a conveyor belt), I was not just exhausted from talking so much; I was desperate to see something that I wouldn't have seen on the New Jersey Turnpike besides the occasional black cab.

"There's a mailbox!" I yelled as we finally turned onto an ordinary street and came to a sudden stop. "Oh, my God! Look! A double-decker bus!"

"Why, so it is," said Caroline.

The bus moved, and we inched forward.

Robert muttered, "Bloody traffic."

I leaned my head against the window so I wouldn't miss anything (though at the speed we were going, I'd pretty much have had to shut my eyes to miss anything bigger than a gnat). I guess I had this picture in my mind of narrow, cobbled streets lined with quaint little stores from seeing

A Christmas Carol about five hundred times. But the streets we went through weren't anything like that. They looked just like regular streets, and the stores were all regular stores, too: McDonald's . . . Burger King . . . Subway . . . KFC . . . Starbucks . . . the Gap . . . French Connection . . . Foot Locker . . . Tower Records. There wasn't a Ye Olde English Tea Shoppe to be seen. I wouldn't even have known I was in London if we weren't driving on the wrong side of the road.

I turned my attention to the people trudging through the rain. It was all hoodies and baseball caps and sneakers with the Nike swoosh on the side. There wasn't a good suit or bowler hat in sight.

What did they do with London? It's as if they've moved part of America and stuck it here. I could only hope that they'd put London in Putney.

Robert finally turned onto a wide road lined with houses on either side.

I had two images of London houses. The first was those big, fancy white houses with wrought iron fences and tiled stoops like where Oliver Twist's grandfather lived in the movie. The other was those narrow, gray houses like where the Cratchits lived. But the houses on this road didn't fit either of those images. They were all two stories high, with a tiny porch over the front door, a bay window beside it, and a tiny garden crammed with shrubs and flowers between it and the sidewalk. It was more like something you'd find in the suburbs—except that these houses were all attached and there weren't any statues of the Virgin Mary out front. If this was Putney, it wasn't where they'd put London. And it wasn't anything like the dead cool city Kev told me about with the markets and the street life and all that stuff either. It looked like the most exciting thing that happened around here was when the hedges got trimmed (probably every week). I started hoping that we were just taking a detour to avoid another traffic jam.

Halfway down the block, Robert stopped the car.

"Here we are at last!" cried Caroline. She sounded so relieved, you'd think she'd been away from home for months. "That's our house, number twenty-two."

Number 22 looked exactly like number 20 and number 24 except for the color of its front door (which was gray and not black or dark blue).

"It's really nice," I said. Which it was. It didn't exactly make you think that Charles Dickens was going to come strolling along (or even Orlando Bloom, unless he was lost), but there wasn't any peeling paint, or weeds in the garden, or broken steps, or any of the other things that I pretty much associate with home. I figured that if it wasn't raining the windows would be sparkling in the sunshine. "Our house is practically falling down."

"Oh, dear," said Caroline. "That can't be very pleasant."

I'd never thought of it as being pleasant or unpleasant; it's just the way it is.

Robert opened his door. "Why don't you show Cherry her room, Caroline? I'll bring her bags up after I've checked my machine." He looked back as he got out to give her a big smile. "And then we can all have a nice cup of tea."

At last—a nice cup of tea! Eat your hearts out, all you poor saps back in Brooklyn with your cans of Coke and your cappuccinos. I was going to have a nice cup of real English tea.

Robert had already disappeared up the stairs by the time Caroline and I got to the front door.

Caroline stepped inside first. "I'm afraid it's in a bit of a state. But things have been rather frantic lately. . . ."

Caroline's mother had hurt her back so she had to look after her, and then there was Sophie's trip to get ready, and, wouldn't you know it, the cleaner was on holiday too. None of these things really add up to *frantic* in Brooklyn (where the cleaner is what you put in the bucket to mop the floor!). Frantic is when you can't pay the rent and they've turned the electricity off again and someone left the refrigerator door open and Bart ate everything that wasn't in glass.

I said the house looked OK to me. This was an understatement. By my family's standards it practically looked unlived in. There was nothing piled up on the stairs or the floors. Nothing hanging from the ceiling. The only things on the coat rack were two raincoats. There weren't even any heaps of stuff on the small table in the hall. If it was in a state, it was a state of grace. "At least you don't have to step over any cat crap to get through the door."

"No." Caroline's voice kind of fluttered. "No, I suppose one doesn't."

I looked into the living room. "Wow . . ." I gave the Brooklyn whistle of appreciation. "You've got real furniture."

It was too bad I wasn't making a joke, since Caroline finally laughed at something I said. It wasn't much of a laugh—if anyone had been opening a bag of chips nearby, I wouldn't have heard it—but it was definitely a laugh. "Righty-ho," said Caroline. She hung her bag on the coat rack. "Let's show you your room."

I said I couldn't wait.

There were five doors off the hallway upstairs. There weren't any pictures or anything stuck to them and no blobs where someone with filthy hands or a muddy pig in his arms had touched them. They were so clean, they looked like they'd just been painted. (If my family moved *every* week, our house would never look like this!)

Behind the first door was the bathroom. It sparkled just like the bathroom in a TV commercial.

"Well, that's a relief," I said. "Mr. Scutari said it'd be outside."

This time, when I was joking, Caroline didn't laugh even a little. "Did he?"

Behind the second door was Caroline and Robert's bedroom.

It looked like all they did in it was sleep—and afterward they made the bed.

"Wow . . ." The wallpaper, the curtains, and even the spread were all in the same tastefully dull rose print. "If you had a dress made from that material, you'd be invisible in there."

"Um . . ." Caroline nodded. "I'd never really thought of it like that before."

Behind the third door was the flight of stairs that led to Robert's office in the attic. I could hear him talking on the phone.

"He doesn't like to be disturbed when he's working," Caroline warned me.

"Don't worry," I promised. "My dad's the same way. He threw my laughing Santa out the window when I was little because it kept saying 'Ho ho ho' when he was working. I won't go near Robert unless the house is on fire."

I could hear sitar music playing behind the fourth door.

I said it sounded just like this Indian restaurant we go to on Sixth Street. "Except the restaurant has Christmas lights stapled to the ceiling and all over the windows and stuff." I'd only just arrived, of course, so I could have been wrong, but it seemed really unlikely that there'd be any Christmas lights stapled to any ceiling in number 22.

Caroline said it was Czar's room.

"The Czar's room?" Czar like the king of Russia who was murdered in the revolution? Nobody told me they had royalty living with them.

Caroline blinked. "Oh, no, not *the* Czar. Xar is our son. It's short for *Alexander*."

I'd always thought *Alex* was short for *Alexander*.

"Oh, right," I said. "I forgot you have a son."

"I almost forgot I have one myself." Caroline did another of her impersonations of someone who has to conserve their breath so I'd know she was finally making a joke. "He took a year off to do some traveling, but he's going to Oxford in the autumn. He's always been top of his class. We're hoping he'll go into law—possibly even politics. Robert's always regretted not doing law."

At last here was something I could identify with. "My dad, Sal, he's always felt bad that he never learned to swim and he almost drowned in this flood in Guatemala one time, so he made sure we all learned when we were little."

Caroline didn't hear me. You wouldn't think a person could worry about knocking on a door in her own house, but you'd be wrong. Caroline could. She was staring at the door as though all of a sudden she was afraid of what was behind it.

"Oh dear . . . I wonder if we should bother him." She smiled uneasily at the knob for a few seconds as though she was waiting for it to answer her question.

You really have to wonder how the English managed to colonize most of the world. *Should we get off the boat here? Should we bother them with our military might? Should we take their land? Should we give them blankets infected with smallpox? Should we convert them to Christianity and destroy their cultures?* I mean, really, you wouldn't think any of them had ever gotten out of the house with all this dithering.

"Why not?" I asked. "He's not studying law right now, is he?"

The smile fluttered like a trapped butterfly. "No, no, of course he isn't." She raised her fist and knocked really gently. "Xar?" she called. And then (in case he didn't recognize her voice), "Xar? It's Mummy."

No one shouted back like they would on Herkimer Street.

"Are you sure he's in there? Maybe he just left the CD on."

"Oh, I don't think so. . . ." She made it pretty clear that leaving the CD player on wasn't something the Pitt-Turnbulls do. "And he didn't say he was going out." She gave a few more I-don't-really-want-to-bother-you raps. "Xar? Xar, darling, are you all right?" She lowered her voice. "He really hasn't been the same since he got back from India. One never knows what one might pick up in places like that."

I decided not to tell her that when Sal went to India he picked up amoebic dysentery. She obviously had enough to worry about.

"Maybe he can't hear you. You know, because of the music. Maybe you should knock a little louder."

Caroline knocked a little louder, but by Brooklyn standards she might as well have been hitting the door with a sock.

"Xar? Xar, I've brought Cherry to meet you. Please open the door."

My mom (who you've probably figured out by now has a take-no-prisoners kind of nature) is a major advocate of direct action. She would have kicked the door in by then. It was possible that I was more like her than I thought.

"Maybe if you rattle the knob, he'll notice," I suggested.

"What a very good idea." Caroline rattled the knob, but she did it like she was afraid of breaking it. "Xar, darling? Xar?"

I shuffled from one foot to the other. I'm all for politeness and good manners, but there are limits, aren't there? Even when you're trying to make a good impression. "You want me to try?" And before Caroline could say no, I got in front of her and pounded on the door the way the cops do when they really want to get in somewhere.

Caroline sort of gasped and stepped back as the door swung open.

I stuck my head into the room. There weren't any boxes of Christmas lights stapled to the ceiling, but this was definitely where Caroline's passion for neatness, floral patterns, and color coordination came to a dead stop and keeled over. The walls were covered with Indian fabrics, the bed was unmade, and there were heaps of stuff all over the floor. There was even a shrine on the dresser with a stone Ganesh at the center that had a piece of incense sticking out of his head. Except that it actually had real furniture it almost reminded me of my half a room back home. Hope took hold of my heart. Maybe my summer wasn't going to be all smiles and apologies after all. A regular person lived in this room. Not a particularly neat person, maybe, but a regular one. And I was willing to bet that the Czar wasn't as well mannered and polite as his parents. I bet he shouted and grumbled and stuff like that (if the smell was anything to go by, he definitely farted).

"He's not here," I reported.

"Oh." Caroline stayed well out of visual and olfactory range, so I figured she did know what was inside after all. "Oh, I must have misunderstood. I didn't realize he had plans today. We hardly ever see him anymore. He's in and out like smoke. I suppose he must have a girlfriend. But I did tell him . . ." She sighed. "Well, you'll meet him later, won't you?"

I said I couldn't wait.

Caroline started apologizing about my room before we even got to the door. "I'm afraid it isn't very large . . . and it does look out on the road . . . and it doesn't really have a proper bathroom—just the shower . . ."

51

Not only did I have only *half* a room on Herkimer Street, but it looked out on Houdini the rooster and the only time it came close to having a shower was when Tampa threw a glass of water over me to wake me up. As long as Sophie's room didn't have a litter box or Tampa or Gallup in it, I couldn't give a piece of toilet paper if all it had was a bowl and a pitcher. "A shower's great."

"And there isn't any lock—I wouldn't want Sophie trapped in there with an allergy attack . . ."

Of course she wouldn't.

"That's OK, I'm not used to locks anyway."

"But there is an orthopedic mattress." You'd think she was a real estate agent and I was a prospective buyer. "We wouldn't want Sophie to get back problems in the future."

God forbid.

I felt like saying that maybe she shouldn't have sent Sophie to sleep on my old mattress on the floor then, but all I said was, "Oh, right. Of course you wouldn't."

"And there are blackout blinds. You know, for migraines." Caroline shook her head sadly. "Do you get migraines?"

I shook my head. "Not yet."

Just when I was beginning to think we were going to be standing in the hall for the rest of the afternoon, she finally took hold of the knob. "This"—I held my breath—"this is your room."

There was a bed with feet and a headboard and everything, and a desk, and a chest of drawers, and a bedside table. There was even an armchair—which was pretty astounding to me since we don't even have an armchair in the living room in Brooklyn.

Though it wasn't the only astounding thing about the room. It was just as well I wasn't breathing or I might have screamed out loud with horror and shock.

"Well?" Caroline turned around to look at me — like a real estate agent hoping she's clinched the deal. "What do you think?"

Sky, the woman with a saying for every occasion, would have had one for this: Least said, soonest mended.

I smiled back at Caroline. "Wow."

She interpreted this to mean that I thought it was great—which was what I hoped she'd think.

"Oh, I am glad you like it," she gushed. "Sophie chose everything herself."

"Really? That's amazing." So as well as being insane, Sophie had no taste that wasn't bad. "It's so—it's so—" I'm not usually at a loss for words, but they were all scampering for cover like people caught in a sudden storm. "It's—it's really pi—it's really pretty."

What it was was really *pink*. All of it. The whole enchilada. Walls, curtains, rugs, dressing table, dresser, desk, trash can . . . even the TV and the phone. The only things that weren't pink were the stereo and the computer, but they had pink flowers stuck all over them to make up for that little oversight. *God and all the angels in heaven . . .* I thought. *It's like falling into a vat of Pepto-Bismol.*

"Sophie's cleared out most of her personal things so you'd have enough room," said Caroline.

I'll say she had. It looked like the looters had been in. Except for a piece of notepaper (pink!) taped to the computer with the password on it so I could get online, there wasn't anything anywhere. No pictures on the walls, no tchotchkes on the dresser, no junk piled up on the desk or the bedside table. It looked like a bedroom in Barbie's model home. I seriously doubted that there were any dirty clothes under the bed either.

"And she's emptied half of the chest of drawers." She pointed to the dresser. "And half the wardrobe." She pointed to the closet. "But she did leave them, of course." She pointed to the bed.

I followed the moving finger. The Pepto-Bismol Experience must have temporarily blinded me. There was no other way I could have missed *them*.

I figured the odds favored the bedspread being pink as well, but it wasn't actually possible to see the bedspread because every inch of it was covered. By *them*.

"Gee . . ." The words were ducking for cover again. "Gee, I don't think I've ever seen so many stuffed animals in one place before. Not even in a store." Not that I ever wanted to. It looked like the teddy bears were having their picnic in Barbie's bedroom.

Caroline's smile softened. "I think Sophie was afraid you might feel a little lonely at first."

How incredibly thoughtful of her.

"Gosh, and all I left her was Tampa." *Tampa and my dirty laundry.*

"I do hope you'll be comfortable here," murmured Caroline.

If I had a choice between living in a room like this in Brooklyn and living on the street, I'd have grabbed my sleeping bag and my backpack and headed for the doorway of the nearest church. But this wasn't Brooklyn; this was London, England. What was a little pink and a few hundred stuffed animals in London, England?

"Oh, I will," I assured her. "I'm sure I will. It's great."

With a little luck I'd be asleep most of the time.

A Nice Cup of Tea

What's the first thing that comes into your mind when you think of England? Lots of people would say the Beatles or the Rolling Stones. Other people would say Charles Dickens, William Shakespeare, Jane Austen, or Bridget Jones. Angelina's mother, who worked for an English family when she first got to America, would say that the first thing she thought of was how the English are very polite and never shout, not even when they're so angry they want to stuff feathers up your nostrils. Mr. Young would say good suits, great gardens, and lovely accents. My gran would say stuff like the Clearances, Bloody Sunday, and the Peterloo Massacre. Mr. Scutari would say rain and an appalling lack of citrus fruit. Mrs. Scutari would say bad food and the Queen. Barbee Scutari would say that they speak English. But I figure that most people would probably say tea. Everybody knows that tea's the national drink. According to Jake, the English believe that there's no problem—big or small—that can't be solved by a nice cup of tea. She even has a song about it on one of her old albums. From what I could remember of the song, tea is a cure for everything from the weather to insomnia. I could only hope it would work as well on post-Pepto-Bismol trauma.

As soon as we walked into the kitchen, I spotted the juice carton on the table and the dirty dishes left by the sink. I was pretty sure Caroline hadn't left them there.

Caroline spotted them, too. "That'll be Xar." She shrugged philosophically. "At least I know he ate before he went out."

The phone started ringing before she could begin cleaning up.

Caroline gave it a wary smile. "That'll be my mother." She hesitated for a second, looking at the phone like she was wondering whether her mother knew that she was standing a few feet away from it, and then decided that she probably did. "I'd better answer it. You make yourself at home, Cherry. I'll only be a minute."

I looked around the kitchen. It was no wonder I noticed the juice and the plates as soon as I walked into the room. Our kitchen in Brooklyn is the Chaos Theory given substance, form, and a stove. But the Pitt-Turnbulls' kitchen sparkled and gleamed like nobody actually ever used it—they just cleaned it. And it was really organized—like it had been planned down to the last handle. Not just the cabinets but the appliances (which included more than one that you wouldn't find on Herkimer Street) were all built in. Everything matched. There wasn't one single thing that shouldn't really be in a kitchen (no papier mâché trees or anything like that). It would've been easier for a polar bear to make herself at home than for me to.

"Yes, I know, Mum," Caroline was saying. "Yes, I am sorry, but we only just got into the house."

I glanced over at her, and she gave me a smile. Her fingers were crossed like a little kid's.

I decided to give her as much privacy as I could without actually leaving the room. There was a serving hatch in one wall of the kitchen and I went over and looked through that. On the other side was a real dining room. There was a big, polished wooden table in the middle of it with a vase of roses on it, and there was a carpet on the floor. We don't have a dining room at home (our kitchen table has everything on it *but* flowers), and we don't have any carpet in our house because Bart would eat it and Gallup and Tampa would spill blood and ink and stuff like that on the remains. The Pitt-Turnbulls' carpet looked like no one had ever walked on it, never mind dropped a quart of cranberry juice all over it. It was definitely a room where you dined, not a room where you ate. There were French doors that led into the garden. But what dominated the room was an enormous painting of a large black-and-white cat sitting in a box. In one corner of the portrait it said MR. BEAN 1995, and under that, Caroline had signed her name. So now I knew what kind of artist Caroline was. When Jake does a portrait, she makes it out of bottle tops or labels.

"Yes, Mum, yes, I know, but there was a bit of a delay . . ."

On the wall next to the hatch there was a photograph of the Pitt-Turnbulls in the snow. They were all wearing sunglasses, knit hats, and parkas and holding skis. They could have been in a breath-mint ad. I studied the Czar. The photo looked like it was a few years old, so it was before he went to India and changed, and it was hard to make out his face with the glasses and the hat and everything, but he looked kind of interesting.

"Of course, Mum . . ." Caroline's voice was soothing like a hot bath. "How could I forget about you?"

There wasn't much more to see (a refrigerator's a refrigerator even if it isn't twenty years old and covered with photographs) so I sat down at the table by the window to wait for Caroline to finish apologizing to her mom.

There was a blue-and-white-checked cloth on the table and another vase of roses.

I looked out the window. In Brooklyn we have a backyard, but the Pitt-Turnbulls had a garden. Mr. Young would have been ecstatic. The garden looked like it was melting in the rain, but you could still tell that it wasn't the kind of garden where you throw a few seeds down and hope for the best. It looked as planned as the kitchen.

Caroline sighed. "Yes, I'll be over after lunch. Of course I will. Yes. Yes, I'll ring when I'm leaving the house. . . . Of course I will. I promise."

I looked over as Caroline hung up the phone. "Your mom giving you a hard time?" I figured this was something we could bond on. My mother's always giving me a hard time.

Caroline looked surprised. "Pardon?"

I nodded toward the phone. "It sounded like your mom was giving you a hard time. Jake's always on my case about something. It's really wearing."

Caroline shook her head, and her smile went with it. "Oh no, no, she wasn't giving me—it was nothing like that. Poor old Mum, she's been in constant pain since she hurt her back. It's made things very difficult . . . for her. Very difficult for her."

OK, so mothers being stress machines wasn't going to bond us, but maybe bad backs could.

"That's a real bummer," I sympathized. "My gran, Sky, she threw her back out jive dancing a couple of years ago. She said it was like the tenth circle of hell, only she couldn't even say that she thought she deserved it."

"Really? Jive dancing?" Caroline gazed at me vaguely for a few seconds, probably wondering what jive dancing is, and then she turned up the smile. "Well, now," she said. "How about that tea?"

In my house you help out or you starve to death. I automatically got to my feet. "What can I do?"

"Do?"

You'd think nobody ever offered to help her before, she looked so surprised.

"Yeah. You know. Get out the mugs or put the milk on the table—something like that?"

"Oh, don't be silly, Cherry. You just sit down and relax. You've had an arduous journey."

Arduous? Sitting in a plane? In Brooklyn you have to break a sweat for something to be counted as arduous. But I didn't argue. Being waited on was something I totally wasn't expecting either. I sat back down. I might have trouble getting used to sleeping in Barbie's bedroom, but I figured I wasn't going to have any trouble getting used to not having to do much.

Caroline filled what looked like a plastic pitcher with water.

"You use a pitcher for making tea?"

"Oh, it's not a pitcher," said Caroline. "It's an electric kettle."

An *electric* kettle? What would they think of next?

Then she put a bright yellow teapot on the counter and took a canister that said TEA from the cabinet.

I was fascinated. "I've never seen anyone make tea in a pot before."

"Oh, we never use bags." She smiled at me kindly, the way the Queen does in those pictures of her being given bunches of flowers by small barefoot children. "I'm afraid we're a bit fussy about our tea. My mother always says it's one of the most important symbols of our civilization."

"Really?"

Sky always told me that the most important symbols of English civilization were colonization and genocide.

Caroline nodded. "She says you can tell a lot about a person from the way they make a cup of tea."

"Really?"

I guessed it made as much sense as being able to tell what people are like from the shoes they wear.

If you come from Brooklyn, you pretty much think making tea is only slightly more complicated than opening a bag of potato chips, but British ingenuity had obviously given the world more than the steam engine and the electric kettle. Caroline took me step-by-step through the intricate and mysterious process of tea making that had been developed over centuries as an important symbol of English civilization.

First of all, you *have* to make it in a pot. Then the water has to be *absolutely boiling*. If it's not *absolutely boiling,* all is lost. After the water's boiled, you have to warm the pot. There's no sense putting absolutely boiling water in a cold pot, is there? I said I guessed not. And then after you've

62

warmed your pot, you put in four perfectly equal scoops of tea.

"One for each cup and one extra," Caroline instructed.

I asked if the extra one was for good luck.

"For the pot." Caroline smiled and put a quilted cover that looked like a cat over it. Mr. Young was obviously right. Only a really advanced civilization would clothe its cooking utensils.

"Now what?"

Caroline looked at her watch. "Now we have to let it steep for precisely seven minutes."

What happened if it only steeped for six? Did the world come to an ugly end? Did we give up and reach for the cyanide?

Caroline got three cups and saucers from one of the cabinets and put them on the table. They were as sparkling and clean as brand new.

"Holy schmoly." Would my fascination never end? "We don't even own any cups. We just have mugs." And they're all chipped or broken and have other lives as paint pots and things like that.

The phone rang twice while we waited for the seven minutes to be up.

The first time, I said that Jake never answers the phone when she's busy. "Why don't you just let the machine get it?"

"Oh no, no . . . I couldn't do that." Caroline's smile seemed to have got stuck on apologetic. "It might be important."

It was her mother. It was her mother the second

time, too. She sure seemed determined that Caroline wasn't going to forget about her.

Robert came in as if he'd been summoned just as Caroline started pouring the tea.

"For God's sake, Caroline, what are you doing? Milk first, Caroline." He sat down across from me. "You know that. Milk first. We don't want Cherry going back to Brooklyn not knowing how to make a proper cup of tea, do we?"

"God, no." I laughed. "Nobody'd believe I was really here. They'd think I went to the Jersey Shore and just said I'd been in England."

Robert nodded. "Precisely. There's a proper way to make tea and a wrong way. So don't forget, you must always put the milk in first."

"Only I don't see how it would taste any different," I said. Maybe it was the jet lag, but I couldn't stop myself. I've been raised by a woman who regards sell-by dates as a suggestion. "I mean, it doesn't really make sense that it would taste different, does it?" *Did it?*

Apparently, it did.

"It may not make sense," Robert informed me, "but it's true." He handed me a cup. "You just taste this and see if it isn't the best cup of tea you've ever had."

I put the cup to my mouth and took a big swallow. From the major deal they made about it, I guess I was expecting something that tasted like the nectar of the gods—or at least something drinkable.

"Oh, dear! I am so sorry!" Caroline rushed over faster than a speeding bullet and slapped me on the back. "Is it too strong?"

"Oh, no . . . no . . . it's delicious. . . . It . . . it just went down the wrong way." I wiped the tears from my eyes with the back of my hand. "I guess I drank it too fast—you know, because it's so good."

"There you go," said Robert. "What did I tell you?"

Had I Crossed the Ocean or Fallen Down a Rabbit Hole?

When I went up to my room after my encounter of the third kind with a cup of tea, my bags (OK, my duffel and my box) were sitting in the middle of the floor, where Robert had left them, but it was like I was seeing them for the first time. They looked really out of place. They looked like a builder in his work clothes in the Queen's bedroom. You were afraid they were going to put their feet on the spread or break something just by being there. They pretty much looked the way I felt. Like they'd been beamed down from another planet. It was a planet that was a lot less clean, a lot less neat—and a whole lot less pink.

But there was no point in going into the lonely and homesick mode. So what? Feeling sorry for myself wasn't going to make things better. Things were what they were. What would make them better was to get myself settled. You know, find my space. Relocate my spiritual center. Then everything wouldn't feel so strange and uncomfortable. Besides, I was only going to be here for six weeks, not the rest of my life. And it wasn't like I was in a war zone or anything. Six weeks I could do.

So to start with, I took a shower.

It wasn't a Brooklyn shower (attached to the wall). It just sort of fit into a holder, and instead of regular faucets, it had some kind of dial thing, but I eventually figured out how to turn it on and get hot water and it worked OK—which was a lot more than I could say about the tea.

What didn't work was my hair dryer. I stood there holding it in my hand, staring at the socket in the wall. The plugs were different.

I started to revise my idea of having been beamed down from another planet. It was more like I was Alice in Wonderland. I'd fallen down a rabbit hole and into a world where everything kind of looked the same but wasn't. I figured that one of the really major advantages of Europe over close-to-Europe was that in Europe I'd know I was in a strange country but here everything was vaguely familiar so I didn't think it was really a strange country—only it was. I mean, if I was in Italy I wouldn't understand what they were saying because they were speaking Italian, but in England they spoke English and I still didn't understand them.

I dried my hair as well as I could with a towel and clipped it up, and then I changed into some clothes that didn't smell like I'd had a rough ocean voyage.

Then I unpacked my stuff. I put Gallup's painting and Tampa's box on the bedside table so they'd be the first things I saw when I woke up. I set up my altar to the Earth Goddess on top of the dresser, to keep me safe from the forces of pink.

I didn't know what to do about the bears. Well, that's not totally true. I knew what I *wanted* to do with them (stuff them all into my duffel and stick it in the closet), but I couldn't make myself do it. Partly because I knew I'd imagine them all crunched together like factory hens pitifully calling out to me in the night, and partly because I didn't think Caroline would be exactly overjoyed when she found out what I'd done. I mean, they were Sophie's beloved childhood toys, weren't they? I didn't want to act like they were the natives and I was a colonist.

So I sat them all in the armchair and turned it around so I couldn't actually see them staring at me when I was in bed.

Caroline was setting the table in the dining room when I got downstairs.

"Wow," I said. "Is somebody coming? Sky, my gran, she's got a dining room, but we only eat in it if it's a special occasion—you know, when there's too many people to fit in the kitchen."

"No, it's just us." Caroline shrugged. "I thought it would be nice to have a proper lunch, as it's your first day."

I could only hope her idea of a proper lunch

wasn't anything like her idea of a proper cup of tea.

"Oh, right," I said. "I just thought because there are four plates—"

"Oh, that . . ." She straightened out a fork. "I just thought that perhaps Xar might remember . . ."

Remember what? Where he lived?

Caroline decided to change the subject.

"I have an idea." Her smile had faded for a second there, but now it was back in force. "How would you like to see my garden?"

I could see the garden just great from where I was through the French doors (and through a lot of water), but I could tell that wasn't what Caroline meant. She had the same look in her eyes that Gallup gets when any living creature that isn't a human or a plant comes into the conversation— obsessional.

"Sure." My head was still pretty wet, so it wasn't like I was going to ruin my hair or anything. "I've never seen a real English garden before, but Mr. Young—he runs the grocery store where I got the peaches box?—Mr. Young says they're really something."

Caroline hauled out two pairs of green boots and a floral umbrella from the closet under the stairs.

Caroline stepped through the French doors and opened the umbrella, and I went with her. I could see us as though I was hovering over our heads,

Caroline and her flowery dress and green galoshes, and me in my black jeans and T-shirt and Sophie's green galoshes, and the umbrella swaying above us like a giant bouquet. It was pretty surreal.

"Of course there won't be many birds about in this weather," said Caroline as she stepped onto the stone path, "but we have robins, blue tits, great tits, long-tailed tits, a great spotted woodpecker, jays, magpies, wood pigeons, starlings, wrens, green finches, dunnocks, black caps, blackbirds, red wings, coal tits—we even have parakeets and a sparrowhawk."

"Wow, that's really cool." I tried to sound enthusiastic. "We mainly just have sparrows and pigeons at home. Pancho Villa, that's our cat, he's always leaving dead bodies in the kitchen."

Caroline hummed, "Um . . ." and marched onward.

"That's *Rosa Constance Spry* and over there is *Rosa Brother Cadfael* . . ." Caroline held the umbrella over us with one hand and pointed with the other.

"They're nice." The Alice in Wonderland experience was deepening. I wasn't used to flowers having proper names like people. "They look like roses."

Caroline laughed. "They are roses. English roses. And that's *Laurus nobilis . . . Hedera helix* . . ."

I asked if they had English names.

"Oh, Cherry, I am sorry. I'm afraid I get carried away. Of course they have English names." She stepped gingerly over a puddle. "That's the bay and that's ivy of course. And over there are the rhododendrons and the dwarf conifers."

It was my turn to hum. "Um . . ." I stepped quickly over the puddle, trying to stay under the umbrella.

"And this is the pond." She said it the way someone in L.A. showing you her house would say, "And here's the Olympic-size pool."

It wasn't that much bigger than the puddle, but we stood side by side looking at the pond as though it was one of the wonders of the world.

Caroline pointed out the rocks and the ferns and the grass in case we didn't have any of those things in Brooklyn.

I peered into the gloom. "Is there anything in there?"

"Oh, yes." Caroline's head bobbed, which made the umbrella bob, which made water drip down my back. "There are the frogs, of course. And water snails and the daphnia."

Two out of the three were familiar, which was good enough for me. "Cool."

"Those are the water lillies . . . and the water irises . . . and the water forget-me-nots . . ." With every plant she named, Caroline tilted the umbrella and more water dripped down my back. "And there's the holly . . . the lavender . . . the jasmine . . ." She gave a little gasp of what I can only describe as dismay. "Oh, dear. The wild geraniums are looking rather poorly, aren't they?"

I wouldn't recognize a wild geranium unless it was labeled. But I tried to console her. "Maybe it's just because of the rain. I mean, nothing looks that great in the rain."

"I suppose not." She started walking again, determined that I was going to see every inch of the garden, monsoon or no monsoon. "Foxgloves . . . azaleas . . . willow . . . lilac . . ."

"I've never seen a garden like this. You know, not in real life." If this garden were to take on human form, it would be an army on parade, everybody where they were supposed to be and at attention. It was so neat and orderly that the only thing that looked real was the rain.

"Oh, I am sorry." Caroline looked like an Inuit trying to imagine a world without snow. "Don't you have a garden at home?"

"We have a backyard."

"Oh, I am sorry. . . ."

I was starting to feel like I brought her nothing but misery. I pointed to the tiny house against the end wall. "We've got a shed, though." I decided not to mention that it was made of old doors.

"Oh, that isn't a shed." Now Caroline's smile looked like it was trying to keep up its spirits. "I use it for my studio." She gave a little laugh. "For what my family calls my little hobby."

Hobby? Stamp collecting? Boats in bottles? Knitting? She'd have to be knitting a car.

"My painting."

"Oh, right." Jake is only a part-time artist

because we need to eat and stuff like that, but she would never call it a hobby. She says it's the heart of her life. "I saw the portrait of Mr. Bean in the dining room. It's really cool."

"Thank you, Cherry. Sometimes I worry that it's a bit silly, painting pets." The umbrella and the head both bobbed, and still more water dripped down my back. Caroline sighed. "But there isn't much time for that sort of thing, of course. Even when my mother can walk the dogs herself, there's always so much to do looking after Robert and the children and the house."

I sympathized. "Jake says that's one of the reasons all the really famous painters have always been men. You know, because they never had to do anything else."

"Does she?"

Robert suddenly materialized at the French doors.

"Caroline!" he called. "Caroline. I thought we were going to eat."

She gave me a look. "I suppose one could say the same about writers."

I Meet the Czar Who Escaped
the Revolution

Lunch wasn't exactly the Mad Hatter's tea party (everybody stayed in their chairs and there weren't any rodents in the teapot or anything like that), but it was still pretty peculiar.

There we were in the dining room with a real cloth on the table and the vase of flowers and everything like it was Thanksgiving or something and we had twenty people for this big, fancy meal. Only it was just the three of us and we weren't having a big, fancy meal. We weren't even having something typically English like boiled cabbage or crumpets to celebrate my first day in London.

"This is great." I looked from my plate to Caroline. "I love pizza."

"I thought you might." She passed me the salad. "Make you feel a bit more at home."

The feeling at home thing only lasted for as long as it took me to realize that the cutlery beside my plate wasn't just for the lettuce and tomatoes. (I figured this was another point for Mr. Young and his belief that the English are so terrifically civilized. I mean, how far away from our hunter-gatherer past do you have to be even to think of eating pizza with a knife and fork?)

"Wow," I said. "In Brooklyn we just pick it up with our hands."

"You also drive on the wrong side of the road," said Robert.

"It's so messy, though, isn't it?" Caroline daintily speared a small triangle of pizza. "What with the sauce and all."

I picked up my knife and fork and dug in. A big chunk of pie jumped into the air and landed cheese-side down on the immaculate tablecloth.

"Oh, I'm *so* sorry." (That was Caroline, not me.)

"It's Sod's Law, isn't it?" asked Robert.

I didn't know who Sod was.

"Sod was some poor bloke who worked out that if someone throws you a knife, you're going to catch it by the blade."

"We call it Murphy's Law." (Sky says it *would* be an Irishman who figured that one out.)

"See what I mean about you Americans?" said Robert. "You always have to be different."

After that, Robert went into writer-brooding-over-his-book mode (a state I recognized from my dad, who was once so preoccupied thinking about what he was going to say about Arizona that he

75

didn't even notice that the stove was on fire), so it was left to Caroline and me to keep the conversation going. We talked about the weather and the garden and school and what vegetarians eat and her mom's back and stuff like that. So this was normality. Eating lunch in the dining room with Robert sitting there like he was in a trance and the extra plate and cutlery across from where I was sitting. My gran has a friend who always sets an extra place in case Jesus happens to drop by, which is pretty weird since it isn't like he'd show up because he was hungry, but this was even weirder. It was like the Czar was missing in action for the last thirty years but Caroline still believed that he would suddenly return from the war.

I would've been really happy to see him stroll into the dining room and sit down with us, myself. In my mind, he'd already become the friend I needed. Besides, talking about his trip to India had to be at least a million times more interesting than talking about bean curd and rain.

Even eating pizza with a knife and fork can't take forever (even if it seems like it does), and eventually lunch was over and Robert went back to his garret and Caroline got ready to go to her mom's. She didn't ask me to go along.

"You must be tired," said Caroline. "Perhaps you'd like a lie-down whilst I'm out."

Whilst? Was that a real word? I decided not to tackle it. "Lie down what?"

"Yourself. You know, have a little rest."

I just got there. Why would I want to go to bed when I just got there?

"My gran says you'll get all the rest you need when you're dead," I told her.

Caroline smiled. "Does she?" Then she showed me where anything I might possibly need in the next few hours was. That's the water filter. That's where the glasses are kept. That's where the biscuits live. That's the bowl of fruit. Tea and chocolate drink in there. Coffee in there. Small silver tea ball that looks like an owl for single cups in the spoon drawer. Milk in the fridge. She showed me how to switch on the electric kettle. How to work the coffeemaker. How to light the stove. How to press the power button on the TV. How to work the remote. She left the number for emergencies and her mother's number by the phone.

"Just in case," said Caroline.

Just in case of what?

"Well, you never know," said Caroline. "You have to plan for everything, don't you?"

My family plans for nothing—not even the worst.

"But Robert's here," I reminded her.

"Yes. Yes, he is," she agreed. "But he's working."

Obviously nothing—from earthquakes to invading armies—distracted Robert when he was working (which was about the only thing about him that reminded me of Sal).

After she checked that the garden door was really locked and finally picked up her umbrella and left, I went up to my room to write some e-mails to the folks back home. To Jake to tell her I'd arrived in one piece (not that she'd worry if she didn't hear from me since she knew she'd know pretty fast if I hadn't) and to ask her why she didn't tell me about the smiling and apologizing, and the plugs, and eating pizza with a knife and fork, and the appalling gruesomeness of the tea. To Tampa to let her know that I hadn't run into Harry Potter yet. To Gallup to tell him about all the birds I didn't see in the garden. And to Bachman to see if he'd met the Pitt-Turnbull yet and whether or not she looked like Barbie and was carrying a teddy bear.

I put a CD in the stereo, turned it on, and sat down at the computer.

I was still waiting for it to verify the password when I discovered that my room was right under Robert's office. He started thumping on my ceiling like a demented rabbit.

I turned down the volume.

Thumpthumpthump. "Lower!" he shouted.

I turned it down so low that the only reason I could hear it was because I'd heard it so many times before.

When I finished my e-mails, I realized I had a problem. Like, now what did I do? I'd planned to meditate to relax after all the stresses of the last twenty-four hours, but I was pretty sure that Robert would be thumping on the ceiling again by the third *om*. On the other hand, there was no way I was going to stay in that room with nothing to do but count stuffed animals and shades of pink until I got some answers to my e-mails. So I went downstairs to see if there was anything to drink in the kitchen that wouldn't strip paint.

I found some green tea at the back of the cabinet and put the kettle on.

It was really quiet. In our house the refrigerator always sounds like it's about to take off, but in Caroline's kitchen I couldn't hear so much as a clock ticking. You couldn't even hear the rain. I sat at the table, waiting for the kettle to boil. Being adaptable, I always try to look on the bright side of things, but I was starting to think that it was going to be a really long summer. As dull as waiting in some podunk town in Arkansas for your car to be fixed. I started thinking about camping with Bachman, and the time I tripped and fell flat on my face but my pack was so heavy I couldn't get up again. We'd laughed for at least an hour over that. When the kettle clicked off, I realized that I must've zoned out for a couple of minutes because my eyes opened. And then I realized that it wasn't the kettle I'd heard turning itself off; it was the front door opening, because I heard it being shut.

Looking back on it, I know it doesn't seem really likely, but at the time I thought it might be a burglar. Maybe it was because I was already bored, but I figured that was why Caroline left me all the numbers—because she knew the Terrifying Truth (that even though it looked about as dangerous as a glass of water Putney was actually the Crime Capital of London), only she was too polite to warn me right out. Until Jake got fed up with Sal and moved us to Brooklyn, we lived in a trailer and traveled all over the country (that's how I know about podunk towns with one mechanic who's always fishing). The first thing you learn when you live like that is not to panic. I mean, what's the point? Things are always going wrong. Tires blow out; engines set themselves on fire; you end up in Mexico by mistake. So I didn't panic. I grabbed the cordless phone with one hand and the big frying pan that was on the stove with the other and peered around the door.

A dude wearing a blue hoodie over a collarless white shirt was tiptoeing down the hallway. Just like a thief. Only I knew right away that he wasn't a thief because of the set of house keys in his hand (and because he had a tan that hadn't come from anywhere around Putney—not unless he'd used a lamp). It had to be the Czar. The image of being stuck in a town where the only things that happen are dawn, dusk, and the weather vanished from my head. I'd been right. The Czar was exactly what I needed in my new life. A really cute, young guy who wore jeans and a silver *om* symbol in one ear. He was my ticket out of the sleepy streets of the suburbs and into the dead cool London Kev told me about.

The Czar didn't see me. He was eyeing the top of the stairs like he thought the cops might be waiting for him up there. The cops or his mom.

"Hi!" I put on the warm and friendly smile of the charming, really low-maintenance American teenager anyone in his right mind would want to hang out with. "You must be the Czar."

He was so surprised that he totally forgot that he was on a secret mission. He jumped and hit the table in the hall, and then he turned on me like I'd pushed him or something. "Where the bloody hell did you come from?"

I held up the frying pan. "The kitchen."

He obviously didn't inherit the genetic disorder that makes it virtually impossible for Caroline not to smile. "What's that for? Were you going to hit me with it?"

"Only if I had to."

This didn't make him laugh like it was supposed to. His eyes darted back to the top of the stairs and he lowered his voice. "Where's my mum?"

"She's gone to your gran's." I kept on beaming warmth, companionship, and goodwill at him, even though I was pretty sure I was wasting my positive energy.

"That's all right, then." He sounded relieved. "And it's Xar," he corrected. "As in Alexander. You must be the Yank." He didn't make this sound like a particularly good thing.

"That's right." If I'd smiled any harder, my lips would have split. "My name's —"

"It's some sort of fruit, isn't it?" He turned and started up the stairs. "Strawberry," he guessed.

"No, it's—"

"Oh, I remember," he said without turning around. "It's Cherry."

"Actually, it's Cherokee!" I shouted after him.

"Right," he said as he reached the landing. "Like the car."

"No, like the Indian tribe."

He vanished into his room. That's the trouble with hope, I thought. It leads you on. I was still standing there, gazing up the stairs, when he came running back down carrying a small backpack, a lot like the one that Bart ate. Why is there never a destructo pig around when you really want one?

"Tell my mother I won't be in for supper," he commanded as he strode back down the hall. "Something's come up."

"Sure," I said. "I'd be delighted to." I caught a glimpse of a small red car parked in front of the house before the front door banged behind him. If you asked me, I was right about calling him the Czar. He definitely acted like he thought he was better than everybody else. I stuck my tongue out at the empty hall. "Nice to meet you too, Your Majesty."

After my encounter of the third kind with the king of rudeness, I went back upstairs with my tea. There was an e-mail from Bachman (the friend I really needed) waiting for me. I would've shrieked with joy if I didn't know Robert would start thumping on my ceiling. Bachman said Bruce Lee wanted me to know he was really sorry for barfing all over me like that, and that he wanted me to know that he was sorry for getting on my case about going. *Rain sounds pretty good*, wrote Bachman. *It's already so hot, I feel like my skin's starting to melt.* He was working in his dad's hardware store, which meant he was pretty much sitting at the computer (except when he had to go get somebody some nails or cut a key or something), so I wrote him right back. And that's how I spent my first afternoon in London — e-mailing Bachman in Brooklyn. At least I made *him* laugh. He said he was tempted to go into Smiling Pizza for lunch and ask for a knife and fork. He figured he'd get his picture in the neighborhood paper. He wanted to know if I still wanted him to rescue Sophie from the insanity of my family. *If the cops see me walking around with a girl all in pink carrying a bunch of stuffed toys, they're going to arrest me.* He wanted to know what I was doing over the weekend, since I was missing the Mermaid Parade. *Having lunch with the Queen?* I said we were having a barbecue tomorrow. *Oh, right* . . . Bachman answered. *Now I understand what they mean by the global village.* He cracked me up.

And Then There Was the Queen Who Could Have Started a Revolution

Caroline and Robert were both in the kitchen when I went down for breakfast the next morning.

Robert was staring out into the garden. He turned to look at me over his shoulder. "They used to say that the sun never set on the British Empire, but it's possible that was because it never actually shone on it in the first place." He waved toward the window. "Wouldn't you know it's pissing down?" (How poetic—he wasn't a writer for nothing.)

"Plan a barbecue and you're guaranteed rain," said Caroline. "Sod's Law again."

Or Murphy's.

"Well, all's not lost." Caroline put a pot of tea on the table and a metal rack filled with toast (there really seemed to be no limit to English ingenuity). "We can have a nice family dinner instead. I'll bring Mum round so she can meet Cherry."

Robert rolled his eyes at me. "She means get it over with."

"That is not what I mean." Caroline's smile looked really determined. "Mum's looking forward to this."

I said, "Oh, me too." I figured a normal old lady would be a nice change from my gran.

Robert sighed. "I suppose there's no getting round it." He gave his eyes another roll. "I can't wait."

I was standing on my head (a perspective that made the bedroom look slightly better) when I heard the BMW pull up in front of the house. To tell the truth, I didn't hear the BMW. What I heard were the dogs. One second the only sounds were the occasional muffled grunt or thud from Robert above me or a car passing by, and the next it sounded like somebody had opened the gates of Hell and let out the hounds.

I came out of the pose and went to the window.

Caroline was standing on the sidewalk by the passenger's door holding her flowery umbrella, while two brown-and-white spaniels hurled themselves against her, barking hysterically like she had fresh meat in her pockets.

I'd thought I had a pretty good idea of what Caroline's mother was like. I figured she was going to be one of those sweet, frail, dithery old English ladies like Miss Marple (but probably not an ace detective). You know, in the gray skirt and pastel blouse and an old straw hat with a flower on it.

The kind who's always forgetting where she put her knitting. I leaned forward as Caroline opened the door to see how good a guess I'd made.

I wasn't even close. (Lesson for Today: Don't get fooled by stereotypes!)

"Oh, for God's sake, Caroline!" She barked louder than the dogs. "How can I possibly get out when you're blocking my way?"

Caroline took a step backward and moved the umbrella forward. "I'm so sorry, Mum. I was only trying to—"

"And get that bloody umbrella away from me. You're going to poke my eye out."

"I'm sorry," bleated Caroline. "But you'll get wet."

"It's water!" roared her mother. "Not acid. If you want to be useful, see that the boys don't knock me down."

Pinning the umbrella under her arm, Caroline grabbed hold of the dogs and hauled them back from the car to let her mother out.

Caroline's mother (otherwise known as Poor Old Mum) probably didn't even know what *sweet* and *frail* meant. She was built like a silo. And forget the gray skirt and pastel blouse and straw hat malarkey. She was wearing an electric-blue pants suit, a matching turban, and enough gold jewelry to sink a rowboat. She looked more like some eccentric queen (one who's always giving orders and lopping off people's heads) than Miss Marple.

"Drake! Raleigh!" she bellowed as she heaved herself out of the car on her cane. "Settle down!"

The dogs had been yanking Caroline in all directions, but they immediately dropped to the ground. They knew their master's voice when they heard it.

"You have to let them know you're boss," snapped Poor Old Mum. And she marched past Caroline, who was struggling with the dogs and the umbrella again and trying to lock the car at the same time, and up the path pretty spryly for someone whose back was wracked with incredible pain.

I didn't know if I should just go downstairs and introduce myself or wait to be called. I opened the door to my room while I was thinking about it. I could hear Poor Old Mum in the kitchen. She had a voice that was loud enough to call the pigs in five counties, and that wasn't even when she was shouting. That was when she was just having a conversation.

"Of course I'm not going to say anything," she was bellowing. "What do I care if she looks like Morticia Addams?"

In comparison, Caroline's voice was like the rustle of leaves in the next yard, but I figured that whatever she was saying, the words "I'm so sorry" were probably involved.

"Are you implying *I'm* not diplomatic?" boomed Poor Old Mum. "Have you forgotten that Uncle Farquah was in the Foreign Office? Diplomacy is in my blood."

87

Rustle . . . rustle . . . rustle . . . rustle . . .

"You do exaggerate, don't you, Caroline? It was all a silly misunderstanding. And he certainly didn't start a war. It was nothing more than a border skirmish."

I decided to go down, but I only got as far as the bottom of the stairs when Hell's spaniels came charging out of the kitchen, barking like police dogs trying to tell you that there's a little kid down the well.

"Drake! Raleigh!" Robert appeared in the doorway with a glass of wine in his hand. "Get back here!"

It was just as well he's a writer and not a dog trainer. They kept right on coming. But if you've ever been chased by a demented pig or an aggressive rooster, a couple of dopey dogs are nothing. I stepped to one side as they got close, and they hurtled past me, their ears flapping like they were trying to fly. The first one hit the door and the second hit him.

Robert gave me a wink. "That's one for our side." He waved me toward him with his glass. "Why don't you come on in and meet the owner of the worst-behaved dogs in Putney?"

I said it would be a dream come true.

"There you go!" Robert gave me another wink. "That's the spirit that tamed the wilderness."

Caroline's mother looked even more like a queen when she was sitting down. She was still wearing the turban and she was sort of looming over the table, holding a wine glass and talking at Caroline (who was at the counter, doing something disgusting to a chicken) at top volume. She broke off when Robert, the dogs, and I all arrived in the room. She wasn't a woman to wait for introductions.

"So, you're the Yank," she boomed. "From the Wild West."

I remembered to smile. "Actually, I'm from the Industrialized East."

"I think I could use a top-up," said Robert. "Anybody fancy another drink?"

Caroline wiped her hands on her apron and came over and put an arm across my shoulder. "Mum, this is Cherry. Cherry, this is—"

"Oh, for heaven's sake, Caroline, she knows who I am." She held out her empty glass to Robert, but her eyes were still on me. "You may call me Mrs. Payne."

Otherwise known as Mrs. Pain in the Butt.

I was overcome with gratitude, of course. "Thanks." You can call me Ms. Salamanca.

"So . . ." Mrs. Payne leaned forward, looking straight into my eyes like the Grand Inquisitor. "What do you think of this sceptered isle so far? Is it what you expected?"

Caroline was obviously right. Her mother was about as diplomatic as a nuclear bomb. But I'm used to feisty grandmothers, and I wasn't going to let this one think we read nothing but cowboy novels back in the Wild West. I'd done Shakespeare. "You mean this royal throne of kings, this earth of majesty, this seat of Mars?" I had to hand it to her. She didn't so much as blink. "Well, I think England's—"

"Britain," snapped Mrs. Payne. "We're one country, you know. Great Britain."

Robert opened the refrigerator. "I'm afraid that, technically, Cherry's right, Bea," he called. "After all, we are in England, aren't we? She hasn't quite got round to seeing the entire British Isles yet."

Mrs. Payne made a what-a-revolting-taste kind of face and steamed on as though he hadn't spoken. "Except for Ireland, of course. The Irish always have to go against us."

I decided not to mention the Irish martyrs.

"Well . . ." She tapped her cane impatiently. I was willing to bet she used it even when her back was fine to beat the peasants away. "Have you formed no opinion?"

I felt like saying that since I hadn't even left the house yet my opinion was based on the airport, the ride from the airport, and about twelve hours of gardening shows on TV last night (people in green boots squelching through the mud talking in Latin), but I caught the nervous smile on Caroline's face. "It's not exactly like I thought," I said. "Eng— Britain. It's more like America than—"

Mrs. Pain in the Butt didn't let me finish. "What total tosh. It's nothing like America. We have centuries of history and tradition here, I'll have you know. Centuries. All you lot have is progress. Everything's about tomorrow. You never give a thought to yesterday, you just plow it under like dead leaves."

"If you're talking about the Indians—" I was going to point out that it was the English who started wiping out the Indians, but she didn't give me a chance.

"I'm talking about everything. You people have no sense of the past whatsoever. In this country we respect the past. It means something. It's part of who we are."

I made sure I didn't look over at Caroline. "From what I saw coming from the airport, part of who you are is baseball caps and the Gap and Nike sportswear."

Behind me Robert whispered, "That's two for our side."

Poor Old Mum didn't hear him, she was talking too loudly. "Poppycock. That's just fashion." She banged her cane again. "I'll have you know that I come from one of the oldest families in the British Isles."

Since this last statement didn't really seem like it was connected to anything else, I just said the first thing that came into my head. Which was, "But everybody comes from the oldest family from somewhere."

She gave me a who-is-this-peasant-in-my-throne-room kind of look. "Pardon?"

"You know what I mean. Everybody's from an old family."

"I really must finish the chicken," murmured

Caroline, and she scurried to the other side of the kitchen, out of firing range.

"Not as old as ours," said her mother. "We can trace our line back to the reign of Henry the Second."

I looked over at Robert, but he'd turned his back on us, too, and was busy pouring the wine.

"But in a way everybody can, can't they? I mean it's not like your family's been hanging out here for hundreds of years and everybody else just got beamed down from some spaceship, is it? If you go back far enough, everybody's pretty much related."

Caroline's mother turned to look at Caroline's back and roared, "So where's that grandson of mine?"

Caroline straightened up with a sigh. "I told you, Mum—I doubt that he'll be joining us tonight."

"Won't be joining us?" barked Mrs. Payne. "Why not? Didn't you tell him I was coming?"

Well, there was one reason.

Caroline sighed again. "We hardly see him anymore from one day to the next. I expect he's got a girlfriend."

"Girlfriend?" Mrs. Payne glanced over at me. "Well, I hope she's suitable."

Robert passed by me with the filled glasses. "It's a pity you aren't old enough to drink," he whispered. "It really helps."

Seeing the Sights
and Stuff Like That

On Sunday, to make up for the barbecue, Caroline wanted to take a drive into the countryside and have lunch at a real English pub. I'd seen real English pubs in movies and on TV. They aren't all dark (so you can't see who's in there) and filled with gloomy men like a lot of American bars. They've got lights and pictures on the walls and carpets and women and stuff like that, and there's always somebody in one corner playing darts. I thought the real English pub sounded like pretty good news. But the gods (as usual) had other plans.

"Are you mad, Caroline?" demanded Robert. "In this rain? Are you going to build an ark to get us back home?"

"I suppose you're right." Caroline sighed. "There really isn't any point in driving miles when it's raining like this just to sit in some noisy, smoky room, is there? One wants to be able to sit in the garden."

The "one" that was me would've been happy to sit in a noisy, smoky room, but it wasn't my job to give Caroline a hard time. I figured she had her family to do that.

"I know what we can do," said Caroline. "Robert can take us on one of his world-famous tours." She gave me one of her more encouraging smiles. "Robert's something of a historian, you know. Xar and Sophie used to love his tours."

I wasn't sure what *something of a historian* meant. It seemed to me that being a historian is like being a serial killer—you either are or you aren't—but all I said was, "Really?"

Robert didn't exactly jump for joy at this suggestion. He didn't want to do the tour. He wanted to work on *War and Peace in Putney*.

"You said you'd take today off," Caroline reminded him. "I sorted out Mum early this morning so I'd have the afternoon free."

Robert looked at her like she was a wrong word. "But Caroline—"

"Cherry didn't come all this way to sit in the house watching telly," said Caroline. Which was true. Even if you called it telly and it had hardly any commercials, it was still television, which is generally a whole lot less interesting than watching a leaf blow down the street. "She wants to see London."

As a good guest—and an honorary Englishman—I know I should've said they didn't have to worry about me, I didn't want to be any trouble,

I was sorry if I was being a nuisance, and I was totally jim-dandy staying at home flicking through the four channels. On the other hand, I did want to see more than Putney. I mean, it was already pretty obvious that all the really interesting things that were happening in London weren't happening there. Putney wasn't the throbbing heart of a multifaceted, creative, ever-changing metropolis — it was more like the big toe. Or the nail on the big toe. I might as well be spending the summer in Queens.

"Well . . . to tell you the truth, it would be kind of nice," I said. "You know, to tell the folks back home about. And I did promise Mr. Scutari I'd take a picture of that big clock for him."

Robert sighed. "Well, I can't deprive you of taking a picture of the big clock for Mr. Scutari, can I? I'd never be able to sleep again." He looked at his watch. "All right, group, the Grand Tour sets out in precisely thirty minutes. Umbrellas will be provided by the management." He gave me a nod. "Don't forget your camera."

Apparently, Robert invented the Grand Tour when Sophie and the Czar were little because they wanted to go to places like Disney World like their friends but Robert wouldn't take them. Robert said it was more important to learn about your own history and culture than to have your photograph taken with Donald Duck. I wouldn't have thought it was possible, but he sounded a lot like Jake. The closest she'd ever come to taking us to Disney World was to drive by it shouting, "There it is!"

The Grand Tour headed for the City of London. I thought we were *in* the city of London, but apparently I was wrong. We were in London, the city—and so is the City of London.

"The City of London was built on the site of the first Roman settlement," Robert informed me as he locked the car.

I didn't know there were any Roman settlements in England. It seemed like a long way to go for bad weather. (And it definitely hadn't given the English any clues about how to eat pizza, either.)

"They ruled Britiain for four hundred years," said Robert. And just in case I didn't believe him he dragged us all over the place to show us the remains. We saw a hunk of the old Roman wall. We saw what was left of an old Roman bath. We saw some old Roman tiles. "Try to visualize it!" ordered Robert. "Try to picture what it was like."

But it was hard to imagine a bunch of dudes in togas and sandals strolling around with all the traffic and the modern buildings and planes flying overhead.

After that he took us to see the place where a lot of the early after-the-Romans-went-home city would have been if it hadn't been wiped out by the Great Fire and World War II.

I said I thought World War II was fought in Europe and Africa and the Pacific. Robert said not if you were British.

Robert led us through the rain to the Tower of London, which if you ask me isn't exactly the cheeriest spot in town. There's Tower Hill, where everybody used to come to watch them kill people, and then there was the Tower itself, which if you weren't the king or some friend of the king (or if you'd been a friend of the king but he got mad at you for something) was just a big prison. We shuffled behind clumps of damp tourists to see the dungeons, to see where the rich people were executed, the tower where the princes were imprisoned, rooms filled with tons of old weapons and instruments of torture, and (just so you don't think it's all doom and destruction) the Crown Jewels.

When we came back out, we stood in the courtyard behind a group listening to some dude dressed up like a medieval guard (assuming medieval guards had umbrellas) tell them about who was killed there and when, and how the whole kingdom would collapse if the ravens left the Tower.

I said it must make everyone pretty nervous to have the fate of the country depend on a few birds.

"I wouldn't worry about that," said Caroline. "They've got their wings clipped so they can't go anywhere."

So much for civilization, right?

"This represents nine hundred years of history," said Robert. "Don't you want to take a picture?"

"Not really. I mean, it may be nine hundred

years of history, but it's just the history of the people who ran everything, isn't it?" The ravens were OK, but the dungeons and the Tower gave me the creeps and the Crown Jewels were just rich people's stuff (useless and boring). I mean it's not like any of these kings actually *built* any of the castle themselves, is it? They probably didn't buckle their own shoes. "My gran says the Tower of London is a symbol of the wealth and power that slaughtered and oppressed millions of people all over the world."

"I take it your grandmother's not a monarchist," said Robert.

"Not really. But she's a big fan of Watt Tyler. You know, the guy who led the Peasants' Revolt? I don't suppose there's a monument to him I could take a picture of."

"I doubt it." Robert smiled. "But I can show you where he died."

We saw where Watt Tyler (among a lot of other people) was murdered, and then I finally got to see inside a real English pub. It was well cool. All wood paneling and low ceilings and pressed tin ceilings and old pictures on the walls. Robert said it was at least three hundred years old and that lots of famous people used to get drunk there. I ordered the "Ploughman's lunch" because it sounded sort of interesting, but it was just a hunk of cheese, a hunk of bread, a pickled onion, and some brown glop with chunks in it that looked a little like throw-up. I poked it with my fork.

"It's pickle," said Caroline.

"Ye olde traditional English pickle," said Robert.

I said I liked my pickle green and looking like a cucumber.

I don't know what Sophie and the Czar really thought of the Grand Tour. Maybe they'd liked it as much as Caroline said (they must have been pretty young, after all), but I was hoping that after we ate we could go home. I was wet, I was tired, and I was bored of the kind of history that's about kings and queens and big buildings and wars and how many people were killed that year (for which I suppose I've got my grandmother to thank). I'd rather have seen a house where Dickens nearly starved to death as a child or something like that.

Robert finished off his drink and slapped the glass down on the table. "Next stop: Westminster and the Houses of Parliament," he announced.

"Don't you think we've done enough for one day?" asked Caroline. Her smile was hopeful. "I can't be the only one who's knackered."

But having been dragged away from writing the Great English Novel, Robert wasn't going to let us off that easily. He was in super-guide mode. "Cherry wants to take a picture of Big Ben for Mr. Scutari." He turned to me. "And you could take one for your grandmother, too."

I said Sky wasn't really into symbols of the State.

Robert said she'd be interested in this one. "Not many people know this, but there's actually a small prison cell in the clock tower, where Emily Pankhurst was once held."

"Really? The suffragette? Sky's a really big fan of the suffragettes."

"The very same." His smile was triumphant. "You don't want to miss that, do you, Cherry?"

There was no way I could say no.

"As soon as we get home, we can have a nice cup of tea," threatened Caroline as we trudged past the street where the Prime Minister lives (just a regular house with a couple of cops outside).

I was amazed at how many tourists there were mooching around in the rain.

"They can't stay indoors because of the weather," said Caroline, "or they'd never leave their hotels."

Besides all the tourists outside of Parliament, there was a whole slew of cops and people with signs across the street.

"Looks like Brian Haw's got some company," said Robert.

According to Caroline, this guy Brian Haw had been camped out in front of Parliament for years in a one-man peace vigil.

"They're always trying to evict him," said Caroline. "It's absolutely shocking. They even changed the law to try to get rid of him."

Robert took my picture in front of the Houses of Parliament (me and two dozen Germans), and then I took one of him and Caroline in another herd of tourists. I could only get Big Ben in the picture by more or less squatting in traffic, so I decided to go over to the square across the street to take a really good picture of it for Mr. Scutari. I couldn't get Caroline and Robert's attention to tell them what I was doing because they were huddled over a guidebook with a Japanese couple, but I figured I'd be back before they even noticed I was gone.

But by the time I was across the street, my attention was on the square. I guess that after a day of trooping through the rain to see things that weren't there anymore and jewels and stuff like that, I was up for something really interesting, and the protest pretty much fit the bill. I stood at the curb, Mr. Scutari's picture more or less forgotten, just taking it all in—Brian Haw sitting on a chair holding a big umbrella, and all these people milling around, and dozens of big signs with slogans like STOP KILLING OUR KIDS, and WITHOUT THE RIGHT 2 PROTEST THERE ARE NO RIGHTS, and THERE'S NEVER BEEN A GOOD WAR OR A BAD PEACE.

I didn't even notice it happening, but one minute I was more or less in the gutter, in front of the police, and the next I was on the sidewalk with the protestors. There were a bunch of people with tea lights praying, and some other people singing, and a girl and two guys arguing with a couple of the cops. One of the guys was wearing a blue hooded sweatshirt that looked kind of familiar and the other had on a multicolored, crazily patterned jacket and a cowboy hat. The girl had hair the color of Santa's suit and was wearing a pink tutu over black combat pants and a yellow rain jacket. It was the girl who was doing most of the arguing.

This is when it got really, really interesting. I finally realized that the guy in the hoodie was the Czar.

I suppose I could have stopped myself if I thought about what I was doing, but I didn't think about it. All I thought about was that even if the Czar hadn't exactly overwhelmed me with friendliness, I'd have a lot more fun hanging out with him than I would hanging out with his 'rents. I wanted him to notice me. So I went straight into guided-missile mode and pushed my way through the crowd.

I reached the Czar and his friends just as the cops had decided they'd had enough of the argument and were trying to get them to move on. I gave the Czar a nod. He was looking right at me, and I know he saw me because he got that shifty, where's-my-mother look on his face, but he didn't nod back.

"I'm asking you politely," the taller of the cops was saying. "Leave now or I'll have you arrested for creating a public nuisance."

"I'd like to see you make us!" shouted the girl. "We know our rights."

(Lesson for Today: Life has to be considered really bizarre when someone wearing a tutu and with hair like a traffic light can remind you of your grandmother.)

"So do we," said the shorter cop. "And we're not asking you nicely again."

"I'm not going anywhere," said the girl, and she sat down. Just like that—she just dropped like a rock onto the sopping wet grass.

The first cop grabbed her arm. "That's enough of that then. You're coming with us."

My gran's saying for this occasion would have been: all hell broke loose.

Somebody pushed, and somebody shoved, and a bunch of other people got involved, and before you could say "Give peace a chance," the whole thing turned into a major scuffle. I saw the Czar and his friends running away at about the same second that the long arm of the law reached out and grabbed *me*.

I said I was really sorry, Officer, but I was afraid he'd made a mistake. "I'm not with the protestors," I explained. "I was just taking a picture of Big Ben. For Mr. Scutari back in Brooklyn."

He gave me a look that didn't exactly define total belief. "Of course you were." He seemed to be working on the theory that one girl was as good as another and started pulling me down the block.

"No, really." I may not have been protesting before, but I was definitely protesting now. "My friends—the Pitt-Turnbulls? You may have heard of him—he's a famous English writer? Anyway, my friends are waiting for me over by that big building."

"The Houses of Parliament."

"Right." At last there was something we agreed on. "The Houses of Parliament. That's where they're waiting for me."

"But you're not there," said the cop. "You're over here."

"That's true. But if you let go of me, I'd be over there faster than a squirrel climbs a tree."

"Only I'm not letting go of you, am I?"

No wonder people talk about the English sense of humor.

I couldn't believe it. Day three and I was going to be arrested. At least my grandmother would be proud of me.

And then someone shouted, "Cherry!" and I looked around to see Robert striding toward me and Caroline trotting behind him apologizing to everyone he shoved out of his way.

"Officer! Just what's going on here?" Robert suddenly sounded like some lord about to throw trespassers off his land. "Could you kindly explain what you think you're doing with this young lady?"

I stood up a little taller, like a real young lady. "You're not going to believe this, Ro—"

The officer cut me off to explain. "I'm taking her in for disturbing the peace."

"But that's ridiculous," said Caroline. Her accent had gotten a little more royal-sounding too. "She wasn't disturbing anything."

But men in authority often have a one-track mind.

"She was creating a public nuisance," said the officer of the law.

"What utter rubbish," snapped Caroline. (Talk about everyone having hidden depths. *And who disguised as Caroline Pitt-Turnbull, a mild-mannered housewife with a love of roses . . . "*) "She was taking a picture of Big Ben." Caroline waved at the herds of tourists with their cameras and guidebooks and umbrellas. "Like those people. Are you planning to arrest all of them for creating a public nuisance, too? I should think you'd be better off catching criminals than harassing innocent tourists."

"This girl is a visitor to our shores," chipped in Robert. "And she happens to be our personal guest."

The cop looked from him to me. Maybe he was just a natural skeptic. Some people are. "Morticia Addams? She's staying with you?"

"That's right." Robert nodded. "I'll vouch for her unequivocally."

Officer Keeping the Peace mulled this over while he looked Robert and Caroline up and down.

"Perhaps it would interest you to know that my mother is in a book group with the Chief Constable's wife," said Caroline.

"Of course she is," he muttered, but you could see that because she looked so straight and respectable and everything he pretty much believed

105

her. The officer sighed. "Right, then. Seeing as she's with you." He took his hand from my arm. "But don't let it happen again."

As he shuffled away to bother someone else, I asked Caroline if her mother really was in a book group with the Chief Constable's wife.

"Oh, I don't think so." Caroline smiled. "But she might be, mightn't she?"

So This Is How the Normal People Live

That night Robert took us to supper in another old pub (it was a relief to know that all the good pubs weren't in the country, since it didn't look like it was ever going to stop raining long enough for us to go there). This one was down by the river.

"It's a small piece of old, vanishing London," said Robert.

The pub was on what Robert said used to be a road of warehouses and factories, but all the other original buildings around the pub had been knocked down to make room for big modern offices and apartments (all glass and steel and truly unattractive unless you're a window cleaner).

It was just brick and wood, and inside it was totally crammed with so many antiques and really old stuff that it reminded me of our house on Herkimer Street (Jake would have loved it—there were even things on the ceiling!), minus the pig and the rooster and the cat (but they did have a dog who liked potato chips). Sitting there all by itself next to empty lots of rubble, the pub reminded me of the way my bags looked in Sophie's room the day I arrived. Stranded and abandoned. But it hadn't admitted defeat. It was putting up a fight.

"Should be called the Last of the Mohicans, not the Cat's Back," said Robert.

The reason Robert took us out was to celebrate our close brush with the law.

"That was a real stroke of luck, running into the police like that," said Robert. He raised his glass. "To effortless research."

"Research?" Sal researches his books, but you'd sort of have to seeing as they're travel books (especially since the series is called Places You Never Thought of Going). I wasn't sure how my nearly getting arrested counted as research for Robert's novel.

"Well, it would have been better if they'd actually thrown you in the clink." Robert took a sip of his beer. "But in the normal run of things, I usually only have contact with traffic wardens, not coppers, so it counts as a bit of firsthand experience."

From the way he carried on if you breathed too loudly when he was working, I'd figured Robert was this big shot literary type dealing with the major questions of life with deep psychological insight and poetic prose. But it turned out that he wasn't writing *War and Peace in Putney*. He was writing a mystery novel. That's what he writes.

Some of them are set in Victorian London (which explains the "something of a historian" thing) and some are set now.

Probably because of the effortless research, Robert was being a regular Chatty Cathy for a change. He went on and on about the history of Putney while we ate, but even though it was pretty interesting I was distracted. I couldn't stop thinking about the Czar. I mean, what was with him? He was like the invisible boy. The only way you knew he'd been in the house was because he always left dirty plates in the sink or the milk out and stuff like that. It was bound to make a person curious. It was pretty obvious that he wasn't avoiding me. As far as I could tell, he had less interest in me than he had in doing the dishes. It was Caroline and Robert he was avoiding. But why? It wasn't like they were high maintenance (like some mothers I could mention). Caroline didn't expect anybody else to do anything in the house, and Robert only came out of his attic for meals. But beside being curious, I was also really irritated at him for running off like that and leaving *me* to get busted. I figured it was time that we had a little talk.

So that night I decided to wait up for Putney's answer to Che Guevara to come home. When I went up to my room, instead of going to bed (even though I was totally exhausted from tramping around in the rain all day), I e-mailed Bachman. He was really impressed that I was almost arrested. *I guess England isn't as boring as I thought.* He said he'd dropped by Herkimer Street a couple of times, but there was never anyone home. He figured Jake must be keeping Sophie pretty busy. *Sod's Law,* I wrote back. *Her idea of keeping me busy is making me work, but as soon as I'm out the door, she turns into the camp activities director.* Bachman wanted to know who Sod was. I said he was related to Murphy. After Bachman signed off, I sat up reading. Eleven . . . midnight . . . one . . . two . . .

But it wasn't the stealthy sound of the Pitt-Turnbulls' only son sneaking up the stairs that alerted me to his arrival. I guess I kind of dozed off because what woke me was the sound of voices in the room next to mine. Had he brought someone home with him?

It turned out that I wasn't the only one who'd been waiting up for the Czar. It was Caroline who was in his room with him. And from what I could tell she was in laying-down-the-law mode. I grabbed my empty water glass from the bedside table and tiptoed over to the wall. (Which just goes to show you that you can learn *some* things from TV—it's not all useless yadayadayada.)

"Just what do you think you're playing at?" Caroline was saying. "So long as you live in this house, young man, you'll behave like you're part of this family, not the spy who's lodging in the spare room."

"Fine," growled the Czar. "Brilliant. Anything else you want?"

110

Caroline said that what she wanted was for him to show some interest in and courtesy to their guest.

(If their guest had pushed any harder on the glass, she would have been through the wall.)

The Czar said I wasn't *his* guest.

Caroline said he was wrong about that. If their food was his food, then he was to consider their guest his guest too. "I think it would be very nice if you'd take Cherry out one day. Show her London. The poor girl's probably already bored out of her mind."

The Czar said that not only hadn't he invited me, but he wasn't a tour guide — that was the old boy's job — and he wasn't a childminder, either. "And anyway," he summed up for the defense, "I happen to be busy." (You could see why Caroline and Robert thought he should be a lawyer. He obviously had a gift.)

"Busy?" Caroline's voice got a little louder. "Busy doing what? Robbing graves? You seem to sleep all day and stay out all night."

The Czar said he was busy doing things.

"Well, why don't you take Cherry with you?" said Caroline. "She'd like to do things, too. And I'm certain she'd like to meet your friends."

The Czar said he didn't think his friends would like to meet me.

"And why is that?" asked Caroline.

"Because she's just a kid." Like I was two or something. "Look, can we continue this episode of the Pitt-Turnbull Family Soap Opera tomorrow? I'm really knackered. I'm turning off the light and going to bed."

Caroline said, "I haven't finished yet."

Caroline had more hidden depths than an iceberg. Because she was always patient and smiling and apologizing for everything, I'd more or less had the idea that she never really got mad. Not like people from Brooklyn, who tend to shout even when they're just having a normal conversation. You know, like she was on a higher, more evolved plane because her family was practically as old as the hills. That wasn't it, though. Caroline wasn't any more Zen than Mrs. Scutari; she just had really good manners. But now she launched into the Czar like a lioness making a kill. He was disappointing her. He was all the things Jake always says I am (lazy, selfish, self-centered, a major slob) and he was making her lose sleep (*not* something Jake's ever said to me). Caroline was worried about him. She wanted to know what was going on. Was it drugs? Was that it? Had he become hooked on drugs in India?

All the while Caroline was steaming on like a runaway train, the Czar didn't say a word. If it was Jake in there huffing and puffing and pawing the ground, I might have thought she'd knocked him out, he was so quiet. Then, when Caroline finally stopped all of a sudden, like her car had run out of gas, the Czar said, "Right. If that's the way you feel, I'm off."

Caroline said, "Don't be ridiculous."

The Czar's answer was to make a lot of noise opening and slamming shut the drawers of his dresser, and then more noise opening the door to his room and slamming that shut. Then he banged down the stairs and out into the night.

I was so surprised by all the un-English drama (wait till I told Angelina's mom) that I was still standing there with my ear to the wall after he'd gone.

That's how come I heard Caroline start to cry.

I Take a Walk

Caroline was back in fully operational cheerful-wife-and-mother mode the next morning, zooming around the kitchen like a smiling robot without a care in the world.

"Sleep all right?" she asked.

I said just great. I wasn't sure if I could just come right out and say I heard her fighting with the Czar, so I looked around like I'd only just noticed that something was missing. "Where's Xar? I thought I heard him come in as I was falling asleep."

"Did you?" Caroline set a rack of toast on the table with a grim smile. "I expect you were dreaming. I don't think he came in at all. He's not in his room."

So that was the should-I-say-something-about-what-happened question answered.

Before I could say anything like I was pretty sure I wasn't dreaming, Caroline rushed off to her mother's because Mrs. Pain in the Butt had a doctor's appointment that afternoon and Caroline wanted to get the dogs walked and everything done before then.

I figured I could try to get something out of her when she got back, but she brought her mom with her. When Poor Old Mum was around, she was pretty much the sun and everyone else just revolved around her. It was all Caroline do this . . . and Caroline do that . . . and Don't you have this . . . and Don't you have that.

We'd just finished lunch (late because I had to go down the street twice—once to get the right kind of bread for Poor Old Mum and once because I had to get her the right kind of cheese) and they were finally getting ready to go when Sophie called. What with one thing and another (like her son storming out in the middle of the night and having to wait on her majesty hand and foot), even Caroline had pretty much forgotten about Sophie by then. I heard her mention me a couple of times, but I couldn't really tell what they were talking about because Mrs. Pain in the Butt was complaining to me about her doctor, but I could tell that although Caroline was being really patient she wasn't apologizing as much as usual, and then she said, "We'll talk about this later," and *hung up the phone.*

"That was Sophie." Caroline turned back to us, smiling. "She's having a brilliant time." She focused her smile on me. "You know, you're welcome to come along if you'd like, Cherry. I feel terrible leaving you all on your own again."

I smiled back. "Oh, that's OK." It seemed pretty unlikely to me that sitting in a doctor's waiting room in London was going to be that much more exciting than sitting in a doctor's waiting room in Brooklyn (which is *not at all*) — not even with Mrs. Pain in the Butt there to liven things up by bossing everyone around. "I was thinking I'd walk around the neighborhood and check things out while you're gone."

The idea of me strolling through Putney on my own opened a whole new world of worry for Caroline. "Oh, are you certain that's wise?"

I said I figured that if I could roam around Brooklyn and Manhattan unscathed, I could probably manage Putney.

"Well . . ." Caroline sighed.

But she wasn't going to let me out without backup. She gave me *two* emergency numbers. Just in case.

I said I wasn't planning to be out that long.

"You can't be too careful," said Caroline. "You never know what may happen."

The woman must have been the poster child for the Girl Scouts when she was a kid. But if it made her feel better, she could give me an armed escort for all I cared — as long as it got me out of the house.

Caroline showed me how to use Sophie's phone. She told me how to get to the "high street," where the shops were. Then she gave me a book of maps that covered *every* street in London. In case I got really really lost. She showed me how to use that, too. She took a ten-pound note out of her wallet. In case I had to take a cab home. I said I wasn't planning to go that far. I said that anyway I had my cash card so I could get some money of my own. Caroline said but what if the machine was empty? What if it was broken? What if it wouldn't accept my card? I took the money. I couldn't stand the burden of having her worrying about me not being able to get any money and then being chased by wild chickens through Putney because I couldn't afford a cab.

The houses around the Pitt-Turnbulls' were pretty much the same as theirs. Some of them were bigger, and some of them were smaller, and some were older, and some were gray brick instead of red, but they all looked like they came out of the same box, if you know what I mean. There were flowers all over the place. If they weren't actually growing in front of the house, they were hanging in baskets from balconies. (I figured the good news was that you never had to water them.)

Eventually I got tired of looking in people's windows (they all had furniture) and at their gardens (no rusting cars or broken appliances) and headed for the high street.

I thought maybe it was called the high street because it was on a hill or a bridge or something like that, but it was just the main drag. There were a couple of stores I'd never heard of before, so I figured that maybe they were actually "British," but there was a McDonald's, a Pizza Hut, a

Starbucks, a KFC, a Benetton, and a Gap, which definitely weren't.

The people all looked pretty much like they'd come out of the same box as Caroline and Robert, too. You know, like their kitchens all matched and there wasn't any junk in the back of their car.

I got my money out of the machine without being mugged, kidnapped, or attacked by wild chickens, and was standing there wondering what to do next when who do I see slouching through the rain but Alexander Pitt-Turnbull in his blue sweatshirt with the hood up. He was carrying a bag so I figured he must've gone back to the house to get things he forgot when he stormed out last night.

The Czar was walking in my direction on the other side of the street. He turned into the train station.

There are people (like Caroline) who always think things through. Before they do anything—no matter how big or how small—they imagine every possible outcome of every possible action, and then they decide what to do based on all that thinking because they assume that means that nothing's going to go wrong. And then there are people (like my mother) who pretty much see thought as the enemy of action. Jake says that things almost always go wrong no matter how much you think about them, so you might as well just go for it and deal with the consequences when they actually happen.

I had money in my pocket, a cell phone, and a map of every street in London, so I couldn't see any reason for not following him. This was my chance

118

to see where the Czar slunk off to all the time. I went for it.

There were two or three people hesitating at the curb because the little green man at the crosswalk was flashing. I ran past them and straight into the road. I charged into the train station. I could see the back of the Czar's head going down the staircase on the other side of the turnstiles. The woman in front of me at the ticket booth bought a round-trip to someplace called Waterloo. I bought one too. I was a little shocked at how much it cost (I could have had two rides on the subway *and* lunch for that back home!), but I didn't have time right then to start worrying about my budget.

I more or less vaulted down the stairs and into the train just before it pulled out.

The car was pretty full for the middle of a rainy afternoon—but it wasn't full of Pitt-Turnbulls. I couldn't see any reason for marching through every car until I found him, so I stood by the door. Every time the train stopped, I stuck my head out to see if the Czar was getting off.

He got off at Waterloo. Since that's what it said on my ticket, I took this as a sign. I was doing the right thing. I got off too.

In case you think that Waterloo is only an ABBA song or a battle, I can tell you that it's also a train station. A really big one.

This was definitely more interesting than the high street. There were people rushing all over the place—and a lot of them looked like they probably

119

didn't have a kitchen, never mind one where everything matched. I could tell I was really starting to get the hang of being English, because, whenever someone walked into me, I said I was sorry.

The Czar slipped through the crowds like he slipped through his home (you know, like a ghost), and I trotted after him.

I was so happy, finally out on my own in the middle of the teeming metropolis instead of back in the house like the Prisoner of Putney, that I think if anyone had offered me a cup of tea, I would've taken it.

There was so much to see that I got a little caught up in my head, I guess, the way you do. I started checking out all the different people (guys wearing turbans, women in saris and chadors, and even a couple of punks) and the building (if you looked closely, you could see that it used to be really old but it was fixed up to look modern) and stuff like that. I was watching the women all wrapped up in black chadors dragging their children through the crowd when, the next thing I knew, I looked around and the Czar had vanished (talk about ghosts). I couldn't believe it. I hadn't taken my eyes off him for more than a few seconds.

I started running in the direction he'd been going, begging the powers of the cosmos not to let me lose him. The powers of the cosmos don't always listen to what I say (having a lot of other things to do), but it must have been a slow day for them because this time they did. There he was! He was at the bottom of a staircase—and with him was the girl with the red hair. She wasn't wearing the tutu today. They were practically standing on top of each other, talking intensely. The Czar looked at his watch and shook his head. Then they suddenly turned and started toward the street.

I galloped after them. I had to battle my way through about eight hundred people all trying to get up the staircase, so by the time I reached the bottom, I was just in time to see the blue hood getting into a bus. It was one of those really long buses that can bend in the middle so they can get around corners. It was sad that my first bus ride in London wasn't going to be on a double-decker, but what can you do? I hurled myself down the street and through yet another set of doors.

My personal experience of bus drivers is that they can often be pretty grumpy. I always assumed that was because they were driving in the insanity that is Brooklyn traffic, but it turns out that it's what my gran would call a hazard of the occupation. The ones in London can be pretty grumpy too. The driver wouldn't let me on.

"You have to have a ticket."

I explained that I didn't know where to buy a ticket.

He pointed behind me. "At that machine over there."

"And you'll wait?" I knew that bus drivers can be tricky as well as grumpy. "You'll wait while I get a ticket?"

He wouldn't wait. He had a schedule.

"But I'm a visitor!" I wailed.

He gave me a look. "I don't care if you're Dracula's bride. You've got to have a ticket."

All seemed dark and lost.

Mr. Young was right, though—the English really are a civilized people, and some of them are kind and generous too.

The man behind me tapped my shoulder. "Allow me," he said. "We can't have our visitors walking in this weather." And he touched this round thing in front of the driver with a plastic card.

The Czar was standing in the middle of the bus. I couldn't see the ballerina of the revolution, but the bus was really crowded so I figured she was sitting down farther back. I made my way up the aisle so I was near enough to jump off when the Czar did, but not so near that he might look over and see me and think I'd been sent to follow him by his mother.

We splashed through the rain, and I kept one eye on the streets we passed and one on the Czar.

But Jake was right: things always go wrong.

I was really starting to enjoy myself when the blue hood turned toward the front of the bus. It wasn't Alexander Pitt-Turnbull. It was some dude who was so pale he looked like he'd been living under a rock for the last twenty years.

This is the sort of thing that convinces me that there's somebody at the controls of the ship of life. I mean, really: what are the chances that two blue-hooded sweatshirts of roughly the same height and build were walking in the same direction in Waterloo Station at the same time on the same day? About twelve trillion to one.

I was still coming to terms with this astounding piece of bad luck when the bus set itself on fire. Smoke started pouring out of the engine.

There were a few disgruntled shouts of "Oi!" and "Bleedin' hell!," but the driver just stopped the bus where it was and told everyone to get off.

After the smoke cleared (more or less literally), I realized I'd lost the map book in the stampede off the bus and had no idea how to get back home. So Jake was right that things always go wrong, and Caroline (otherwise known as Girl Scout of the Millennium) was also right that you shouldn't leave the house without a backup plan. I called her on Sophie's cell phone to ask for directions, and, even though I begged her not to, she came to get me. (Lesson for Today: Be prepared!)

As soon as I got in the car, I started telling Caroline how sorry I was (at the rate I was going, I figured the Queen was going to give me a passport) about getting lost and everything.

"Thank God the fire wasn't worse," said Caroline. "You might have been killed."

I didn't think so. "Mr. Trainer—he was the man standing next to me—said it happens a lot. He said the drivers should be getting combat pay."

This didn't really reassure her. "But it could have gone up like a pile of old papers. What then? What if it had turned into a ball of fire?"

123

"But it didn't. Mr. Trainer figured we were lucky it was raining."

Caroline sighed. "You poor thing. You must have been terrified."

I hadn't been even vaguely scared. Nobody was. Everyone acted like it was the kind of thing you expected. Mr. Trainer said London had had the war and then it had the IRA and now it had self-incinerating buses. It wasn't a big deal.

"But I still don't understand." Caroline shook her head sadly at the traffic in front of us. "Why did you go to Waterloo?"

There was no way I could tell her the truth. (Later, I told Bachman, of course. Bachman said he'd had a similar experience with his Pitt-Turnbull, only she knew he was following her and she wouldn't wait up. She even locked herself in the house and wouldn't answer the door! There was obviously something genetically wrong with both of them.)

"I told you." I gave her my most innocent, sincere, and trustworthy smile. "I didn't have a reason. I just saw the train station and I thought, Why not have some fun? You know, a little adventure. I mean, it's not like I knew the bus was going to spontaneously combust."

"No." She gave another sigh. "Though I don't suppose it would have stopped you if you had."

With Friends Like These . . .

Days passed, but Caroline kept smiling and being bright and cheery as though nothing had changed (you know, like the Czar was still sleeping in his room and leaving his dirty dishes in the sink).

"So has Xar gone away?" I finally asked.

"Away?" Caroline sounded like *away* wasn't a word she knew.

"It's just that I haven't seen any crumbs all over the counter or anything like that for a few mornings now."

"Oh, his usual messes have been there," lied Caroline. "But I clean them up before you come down."

I let it go. I mean, it wasn't really my business. But I noticed that she jumped every time the phone rang or Robert came in the front door. And every now and then, I'd find her just standing in the kitchen, staring at nothing. Once I even caught her in the Czar's room picking up a mug of old tea and bacteria.

"I just thought I'd get rid of any alien life-forms," said Caroline. "While he's out."

It looked like he was going to be out long enough for her to get rid of *everything* in the room, paint it, and rent it out, but I said that sounded like a good idea.

But there was some good news—especially for those of us who were starting to feel a little mildewed. It finally stopped raining on a permanent basis. There might be a shower in the morning or the evening or in the middle of the night, but they'd be separated by hours of solid sun instead of seconds of gray skies. All of a sudden everybody was outside and taking off their clothes. Every patch of green was filled with people trying to get sunstroke and skin cancer. And the streets were haunted by ice-cream trucks playing music that sounded like the theme song for some horror movie where an evil clown doll comes to life and starts murdering everyone.

It wasn't really hot—not by Brooklyn standards (in Brooklyn if you can see the air or if you sweat when you're standing still, then it's really hot)—but by day two everybody was complaining about the temperature and the weathermen started saying we were having a heat wave and worrying that we were going to have a drought.

"You see?" said Caroline. "It's not as if we *never* have any good weather."

She ran around like she was in some kind of housewives' marathon, trying to do all the things she had to do and still have time to work in her garden, but for me it was pretty much business as usual (except that now, besides e-mailing Bachman, I helped do things like wrench weeds from the earth and worry about greenflies). Caroline had been so turmoiled by my trip to Waterloo and the possibility that I could have gone up in smoke like a Kleenex thrown on a campfire that I was sticking pretty close to the hacienda. I figured she had enough to worry about.

We were sitting in the kitchen one morning after breakfast. Caroline was making a list of all the things she had to do before she could get into her garden, and I was finishing my tea and contemplating an afternoon of wrenching weeds — otherwise known as plants in the wrong place — from the earth when the doorbell rang.

Caroline looked up all curious and puzzled, and then she shuffled off to answer it.

"Why, Jocelyn!" she cried. "What a lovely surprise!"

I knew who Jocelyn was. Jocelyn was Sophie's best friend. I leaned over so I could see into the hallway, but the only thing I could see was Caroline's back.

"Come in, come in." Caroline couldn't have sounded happier if one of her gardening gurus had shown up to help her. "Cherry's heard all about you, of course. She's really looking forward to meeting you."

None of this was exactly true. All I'd heard

about Jocelyn was that she and Sophie had been inseparable since they started high school, and as far as looking forward to meeting her went, it was a generic kind of looking forward to. I'd have been pretty happy to meet the Pitt-Turnbulls' dentist by then.

Caroline stepped aside to let Jocelyn in. She was petite and fair and all dressed up like she was expecting to be photographed (though, to my relief, she wasn't all in pink!). There wasn't a hair out of place or a crease or wrinkle in sight. She was so immaculate it was scary. You know, like she was really an android pretending to be a human.

"Cherry! Look who's here!"

"I'm really sorry I didn't come sooner," Jocelyn was saying as she followed Caroline into the kitchen, "but I'm afraid I've been away."

Theoretically, you should never judge a person by the way they look. I mean, just because a man's wearing a two-thousand-dollar suit doesn't mean he's not a nice guy. And just because a girl is really well dressed in a this-season-you-have-to-wear-pastels-floaty-skirts-and-wedges-or-you-might-as-well-be-dead kind of way doesn't mean she isn't a deep, intelligent, and sensitive person. But when Jocelyn said, "I'm really sorry I didn't come sooner, but I've been away," my first thought was: thank God I wasn't counting the days or I'd really have been wasting my time.

Jocelyn had stopped by to see if I wanted to go shopping with her.

"I'm going up the West End," Jocelyn informed us. "I thought Cherry might want to come along." She gave a little shrug of apology, more or less in my direction. "I know it's not Fifth Avenue, but it's still pretty cool."

Not Fifth Avenue? I was pretty sure she meant Fifth Avenue in Manhattan (a place I only go to on the way to somewhere else), not Fifth Avenue in my neighborhood (which specializes in dollar stores instead of designers). Why would she say that? To me? Why would *I* care about Fifth Avenue? I mean, look at me. Even when I dressed up, I hadn't worn anything with a name or a logo on it since kindergarten, but today, because I'd been planning to spend the morning digging around in the garden, I was wearing my old black jeans, a ratty old CONFORM OBEY CONSUME T-shirt Sky gave me one Christmas and my No Sweat high-tops. She was either nuts or legally blind.

I said I'd love to go. I figured that if you swap lives with someone, you don't just get her pink room, her teddy bears, and her crazed family—you get her best friend, too.

"I've never known anyone who was into Goth before," Jocelyn said as we walked to the subway. "I can hardly believe it. You really do look like Morticia Addams, don't you?" Her eyes moved from my feet up to my head. "Well, except for the clothes. She always wears a dress, doesn't she?"

This was when I realized that Jocelyn hadn't just

turned up unbidden. Caroline must have been so worried that I had nothing to do that she called in the cavalry.

I smiled back. "More like her daughter."

Jocelyn laughed pretty heartily for someone on whom dust clearly never settled. "Oh, my God, you Americans are so funny. . . . I feel like I'm in an episode of *Friends*."

Which was more than I could say. (Unless it was The One Where Cherokee Wishes She'd Stayed Home and Helped Caroline in the Garden.) We hadn't even gotten into the station yet and already I had a feeling that the afternoon wasn't going to make me really glad I wasn't in Brooklyn. If Jocelyn was the cavalry, I'd really rather take my chances with the Indians.

She turned right off the bridge. "I can't tell you how shocked I was when Sophie said she was going off to New York all on her own without Mummy and Daddy this summer." Jocelyn's voice went squeaky when she said "Mummy and Daddy," like she was about three. We walked down some stairs. "And I'm not the only one. Everyone was shocked. I mean, that isn't like Sophie at all."

"It isn't?"

"You should probably get a travel card." Jocelyn sailed into the station. "Do you know how to use the machine?"

What was she, my mother? (Well, not *my* mother, but somebody's.) *Select Ticket Type*, said the instructions. *Insert Coins*. I thought I could

130

probably figure it out, but I decided not to change the outrageous amount into dollars so I didn't actually scream out loud.

"Anyway, Sophie's just not the sort of person to go off on her own like that . . ." she went on. "Sophie's . . . well . . . I mean, she's my best friend and all and I love her dearly, of course, but she isn't exactly the adventurous sort, if you know what I mean."

I looked over at Jocelyn, a girl who definitely gave the impression that her idea of adventurous was going out with a run in her tights. How on Earth would *she* know?

"She isn't?"

"Oh, puh-lease . . ." Jocelyn sniggered. "You really don't have any idea what she's like, do you?"

I gave her my best Brooklyn, eat-cold-pizza smile. "It'd be a little difficult, seeing how I never met her."

Her smile twisted in sympathy. "And who'd tell you, right?" Only Sophie's best friend, apparently. "Let me put it like this: if life was a funfair, Sophie'd spend most of her time wondering what rides to go on, and in the end she wouldn't get past the carousel. Plus, she wouldn't even get on a horse — she'd sit in a chair."

What a great friend. I was surprised Sophie could bear to be parted from her for even a day.

"Really? Not even a stationary horse? Not even a llama?"

"Absolutely." (I swear, not one hair moved out of place when she shook her head.) "I mean, don't get me wrong, Sophie's a terrific person and an absolutely brilliant friend and all, but she is truly hopelessly—"

Betrayed? Deluded? Unlucky in her choice of friends?

"Dull." Jocelyn's laugh ricocheted around the empty platform. "There. I said it. She's dull. She's a very sweet person, but she's about as exciting as porridge." She treated me to a view of sixteen years of really good dental work. I'd have to remember to tell Mr. Scutari he was wrong about English teeth. "Personally, I blame her mother."

I could tell that all the hours Caroline and I had spent collecting snails and taking them to the nearest park and stuff like that had made us bond because this statement really irritated me.

"You do?"

"Oh, absolutely. She's very overprotective." She flashed the teeth again. "Don't you think so?"

I smiled back as the train pulled in. "I can't say I've noticed."

"Oh, puh-lease . . . You can be honest with me. You've been here awhile now—you have to have noticed. She never stops fussing. *What if this? What if that?* And don't tell me you haven't seen the blackout blind. Really, it's enough to drive you bonkers."

It wasn't the only thing.

Jocelyn strode ahead of me onto the train.

132

"Personally, I think going to New York was the best thing Sophie could have done."

"Me too," I said as I followed her on. "Me too."

As soon as we sat down, Jocelyn said, in this mega casual, could-you-pass-the-salt way, "Did I tell you we're meeting my boyfriend?"

Despite the fact that she looked programmed, she was obviously a girl of surprises. Hidden depths again. I looked at her smile (about as genuine as a two-dollar bill). OK, maybe it wasn't hidden depths. Maybe it was just hidden shallows packed with coral reefs.

"Your boyfriend? No. No, I don't think you did." You were way too busy dissing your best friend.

"Really? Oh, I thought I had. He's meeting us at Oxford Circus."

"We're going to the circus? I thought we were going shopping."

Except that she didn't really look like she actually performed the usual bodily functions, Jocelyn laughed so hard I thought she was going to wet herself.

Not the kind of circus with clowns, obviously.

"Oh, you are so funny. I must remember that one. I really must." She brushed an invisible speck of dust from her skirt. "Anyway, as I was saying, Daniel's meeting us at Oxford Circus." Jocelyn smiled as though she was about to tell me a secret. "I am so certain he's going to love you. I told him you wouldn't be anything like Sophie."

And what did that have to do with the price of dog food?

"Why would he care if I'm like Sophie or not?"

"Well . . . you know . . ." Jocelyn shrugged. "He did sort of go out with her for a bit. Not that it could ever have lasted, of course. Talk about chalk and cheese."

I decided to skip the chalk and cheese and go right to the other part that confused me. "Sophie used to go out with Daniel?" I was about to meet Ken.

"As I said, for a bit. But they were completely wrong for each other. It was like a tiger going out with a hedgehog."

I was trying really hard to get through the chalk and the cheese and the tiger and the hedgehog and keep up with this conversation. "Oh, so you mean they had a couple of dates . . ."

"Not precisely." Jocelyn gave another shrug. "I suppose they went out together for nearly a year. Give or take a month or two."

"Nearly a year? It took him nearly a year to realize she was boring?"

"He's a nice bloke," said Jocelyn. "He didn't want to hurt her."

I didn't think I needed more than one guess as to who it was that helped him overcome that feeling. "Oh, he sounds like a really nice bloke." I smiled. "I can't wait to meet him."

Daniel was waiting by the ticket booth. He was definitely Ken. He was thin and fair and good-looking in an average, uninteresting kind of way. He was almost as eerily immaculate as Jocelyn. You could tell his mom ironed his clothes. He was the kind of guy you could picture middle-aged — like he'd never really been young.

As soon as Jocelyn went through the turnstile they were all over each other like skin cream.

I stood there, watching the masses of travelers swarm around us, while Jocelyn and Daniel made a big deal of demonstrating how crazy they were about each other. I'd rather have watched fish spawn. Poor Sophie, no wonder she'd been so desperate to get out of London.

It's not only good things that have to come to an end — bad things do, too (it just seems to take so much longer — in this case about a million years). But eventually, they had to come up for air.

"Daniel . . ." Jocelyn moved to one side as though she'd been hiding me behind her back. "Daniel, *this* is Cherry." She kissed his cheek. "Didn't I tell you she wouldn't be anything like Sophie?"

Daniel grinned. "I'll say she isn't."

"Cherry, this is Daniel."

"Actually," I said, "it's Cherokee."

"Cherokee?" Jocelyn repeated. "You mean like the car?"

"No." I shook my head. I could hear my earrings jingle. "Cherokee like the native people."

"Oh my God!" shrieked Jocelyn. "That is too much." She gave Daniel a squeeze. "Did you hear

135

that? She's called after a tribe of red Indians. How American is that?"

"That's cool," said Daniel. "Jocelyn here was called after her grandmother."

Jocelyn laughed. "At least no one would ever think I was named after a car."

Though they might think she was named after some kind of snake.

"Right." Daniel put his arm around Jocelyn's shoulder. "Let's get out of here."

I followed them through the lobby and up the stairs. (Lesson for Today: You can't actually walk through a crowded subway station with an entwined couple because they walk slower than everyone else and they take up too much room.)

We came out on Oxford Circus (which, in less civilized countries, is just an intersection). Oxford Street itself looked pretty much like an incredibly busy London street, lined with enough typical American restaurants and stores to make me feel at home.

"Top Shop first," said Jocelyn.

We went to Top Shop first. Daniel and Jocelyn stayed in joined-at-the-hip mode as we walked around. The going was slow since every few feet they'd have to stop to kiss, and sometimes they'd get so involved with each other that it was hard to tell without looking if they were making out or drowning. After Top Shop we went to H&M. Then we went to Miss Selfridge. Then we went to French Connection. Now and then Jocelyn would stop to look at something. Was this *in*? Was that her color? Would those pants make her look fat? Would that skirt make her ankles look thick? I didn't see what it mattered. All the stuff looked pretty much the same. Daniel had Jocelyn to keep him awake, but trailing behind them, I more or less went into a coma. I started thinking about the suffragettes. Besides being imprisoned inside a clock, the suffragettes chained themselves to the gates of Parliament . . . they marched in the streets . . . they were ridiculed and reviled . . . beaten and even killed. I wondered, if they'd known that they were going through all that trauma and torment for girls like Jocelyn, if they'd have bothered. When she remembered I was behind them, Jocelyn would ask me something about New York styles and what everyone was wearing and things like that, but she finally must have realized that I could only have cared less if I'd been dead, and gave up.

It took about a hundred years and just as many stores, but at last Jocelyn found something she wanted to try on.

"I won't be long," she promised. She gave Daniel yet another kiss. God knew how she managed to stay alive before she stole him away from Sophie. "You can tell Cherokee all about our camping trip while I'm gone."

How lucky could one girl be?

As soon as she disappeared into the dressing room, Daniel turned to me with a big grin. But instead of saying, "We put up our tent and then we blew up our mattresses," he said, "You know, Jocelyn's going away the day after tomorrow."

I said, "Oh, really?"

He nodded. "Yeah, she's going to visit her nan. So I was thinking . . ."

There are first times for everything.

"You know . . ." He stuffed his hands in his pockets. "If you wanted, I could show you round a bit."

"Show me round what?"

"Well, you know, round London."

I wasn't sure what he was getting at.

"I've already seen Big Ben and stuff like that."

If he'd jammed his hands any farther in his pockets, they'd have touched his knees.

"Or we could go to a film or something."

"Go to a film?"

He more or less rocked on his heels. "Yeah, you know. A movie. It must be pretty boring for you at the P-Ts . . . you know, coming from New York and all."

"Oh, it's not so bad. I've been helping Caroline dig a canal in the garden."

He stared at me for one of those really long nanoseconds and then he laughed. Heartily. "Oh, right. Ha, ha, ha. That's really funny." He rocked a little more. "You know, there's a Goth club down the other end of Oxford Street. We could go there if you'd like."

Go to a Goth club with Ken? Had every pigeon in London been turned into a pig?

"I'm sorry, but I'm a little confused here. Are you asking me out like on a date?"

Daniel pulled his shoulders up so high that for a second he looked like he had no neck. "Well, it wouldn't be a real date, would it? You know, you're only here for a few weeks."

"So it wouldn't really count?"

"If you say so." He grinned. "But it'd be a good idea not to say anything to Jocelyn about this. She can be a bit possessive."

I'd never realized before how thin the line between charm and slime really is.

I was saved by the reappearance of Jocelyn outside the dressing room with the skirt on. She twirled around so we got the full effect. "What do you think?"

Not a lot, really.

"I'll ring you," said Daniel, his smile on Jocelyn.

"That'd be brilliant. I'd really like that."

I'd rather stick toothpicks in my ears.

Things Change Suddenly, the Way Things Do

A couple of days after my encounter of the third kind with Jocelyn and Daniel, I went down for breakfast to find Robert alone in the kitchen. This was such a really unusual thing that my first thought was that Caroline had finally had enough and run away from home, too. He had half the drawers and cabinets opened and was crouched down, looking under the sink like he'd suddenly taken up plumbing (either that, or he was looking for a bomb).

"Cherry!" He'd never looked so happy to see me. "I don't suppose you know where we keep the coffee?"

Welcome to the weird and wonderful world of Robert Pitt-Turnbull.

"It's in the freezer."

You could see him thinking *What's it doing in there?,* but all he said was, "Right." He got to his feet and went to the fridge.

I filled the kettle. I was starting to get used to the tea. (Steep no more than three minutes and put the milk in last, so you could see how much you needed.)

Robert turned on the coffeemaker, and then he looked in the bread bin (he couldn't miss that—it said BREAD on it in big letters). He lifted out a loaf of unsliced bread and put it on the cutting board like it might explode.

After a few minutes of hacking away at it, he had a pile of crumbs.

"Bloody hell . . ." he muttered. "This is the twenty-first century, for God's sake. Why can't we have sliced bread like everyone else?"

One of the advantages of having a grandmother like Sky is that she's always baked her own bread, meaning that you pretty much learned how to slice it as soon as you could handle a knife without stabbing yourself or else you didn't ever have any bread. So I could have taken pity on Robert and cut him a couple of slices, but I figured that in the twenty-first century, a highly evolved human adult male should be able to cut his own bread. "So where's Caroline?"

Caroline had a bit of a migraine.

"A migraine?" I knew that migraines can be caused by stress. "Is that because she's worried about the Czar?"

Robert looked from the rubble to me. "Xar? She's worried about Xar?"

Obviously, you had to be a character in his book to get his attention.

"Yeah. You know, because he's moved out?"

"Xar's moved out?"

It was like talking to a parrot.

"Caroline didn't tell you?"

Robert frowned, trying to remember whether he knew this or not. "Well . . . she did say they had a bit of a spat and he stormed out of the house."

The man was totally oblivious.

"They did. And he hasn't been home since."

"He'll be back," Robert assured me. "As soon as he runs out of money. And I'm certain that has nothing to do with Caroline's migraine. It's more likely to be all that rain we had." He waved the knife over the loaf, as though he was hoping it had figured out what it was supposed to do. "She'll be down as soon as she's feeling better."

"What if she doesn't?"

"Pardon?"

"What if she doesn't feel better? I mean, what do we do about supper and stuff like that if she doesn't come down?" Robert's one of those people who doesn't think he's eaten if he hasn't had something that used to have parents. There was no way I was cooking dead flesh for him.

He tapped the instrument of destruction (otherwise known as the bread knife) against the cutting board in a pensive way. "Don't worry," Robert assured me. "She'll be fine. And if not, I'm perfectly capable of seeing that we don't starve."

Since he couldn't slice bread or find the coffee, I wasn't exactly convinced of that. "You sure?"

"Of course I am."

Caroline didn't come down.

After Robert went off to work and I'd waited awhile, I went up to see how Caroline was for myself.

The room was so dark it could have been anybody in incredible pain lying on the bed.

I asked if there was anything she needed.

"A new head. If my mother rings, tell her I'll be over later with the shopping."

I said that sounded pretty unrealistic. "You can't even sit up. If you tell me what she needs, I'll get her groceries and walk the dogs."

"Oh, I couldn't ask you—"

"You didn't ask. I volunteered."

Caroline was right about Poor Old Mum not liking change. She was more resistant than a mountain.

She stood in the doorway with her arms folded in front of her like she was going to block me if I tried to get past her. "I don't know about this." The way she was looking at me, you'd think I was a stain on the carpet. "It's a long way for you to come on foot."

"I enjoy the walk. I like to look at all the old buildings and stuff."

She kept on eyeing me dubiously. "And I like things done a certain way."

Wow, what a surprise.

"So tell me how you want them done, and that's the way I'll do them."

She glanced down at the heads poking out from around her legs. "But Drake and Raleigh don't really know you."

"They'll get over it. We've got a pig, a cat, and a rooster at home. I'm good with animals."

"But what if something happens? What if I fall again?"

"If I can't pick you up I'll send a smoke signal and get an ambulance." She could argue all she wanted; she didn't have a choice. "Look, Mrs. Payne, it's me or nothing. Caroline can't do it. She can't even get out of bed."

Mrs. Payne sighed the sigh of a stubborn woman who knows when she's beat. "Well, I suppose it's just for today . . ."

"Right," I said. "So now can I come in?"

Caroline's mother, Drake, and Raleigh all followed me into the kitchen.

"I hear you nearly got arrested," said Mrs. Payne as I started to unpack the stuff I'd picked up on my way over.

I was going to make a joke of it, in case it was a problem for her, but she didn't give me a chance.

"I was arrested once myself, you know."

I turned around pretty quickly. "You?" It was hard to imagine. I mean, obviously people in England are arrested all the time — but not people like Mrs. Pain in the Butt. What for? Impersonating the Queen?

144

She nodded. "At an air base."

"You were in the air force?"

"No, of course not. I was in CND."

"I don't know what that is."

"Well, that doesn't surprise me." Mrs. Payne snorted in a trust-the-yanks way. "It's the Campaign for Nuclear Disarmament. We were demonstrating."

More hidden depths.

"So what happened? Did they put you in prison, or did they just hold you till you cooled down?"

But this wasn't a question that was about to get answered.

She stared at the stuff I'd put on the counter. "What's that?" She took up a small, black cardboard box and held it out at arm's length as though it was seething with maggots.

"It's tea."

"But this isn't *my* tea."

Like she owned the company or something.

"I know," I said. "They didn't have it."

"They didn't *have* it?" It was obviously the end of life as we know it. "What do you mean, they didn't have it?"

I went back to the unpacking. "I mean there wasn't any in the store. They're out of it. So I got you what they did have."

Mrs. Payne was having a really hard time coming to grips with this news. She just kept staring at the box as though she was thinking, *But why doesn't the sun shine? Why don't the birds sing? What happened to the grass?*

"I've been drinking Earl Grey tea for over sixty years," she informed me.

"Right. Then maybe it's about time you had a change."

She started peering over all the things on the counter. "And where are my chops? Don't tell me they'd run out of them as well."

I pointed to a package wrapped in white paper and sealed in a clear plastic bag. "I got you fish instead."

"Fish? You got me fish? But I didn't ask for fish. I asked for chops."

"You shouldn't be eating meat. Caroline talked to Jake last night and—"

"Jake?"

"My mom? Caroline talked to my mom last night and Jake says meat's one of the worst things for a bad back. Because it has uric acid."

"I see." She gave me a sarcastic smile. "And is your mother a doctor now?"

"No, but she learned a lot when my gran threw her back out jive dancing."

"Jive dancing."

"Uh-huh. But she's OK now."

"Well, that's a great relief, isn't it?"

I took the last thing from the shopping bag and put it on the counter. "And Caroline bought you this." This wasn't true. I happened to see it in the window of the bookstore as I went past. I figured

146

it was just what the old pain in the butt needed. Robert wasn't the only one who had to start taking care of himself.

"What's that, then?"

It was pretty self-explanatory since the title gave it away the way the word *cornflakes* on a box of cereal does, but I told her anyway. "It's a book on nutritional healing. It's got a whole section on back pain. All the things you can do to make it better."

She sighed as though of all the pain she'd suffered, this was the worst. "I suppose your mother recommended it," she said.

Mrs. Payne drew me a map to show me where to take the dogs (you could see where Caroline got it from). Apparently, Caroline usually took them for the long walk to the common.

I said, "Common what?"

Mrs. Payne made one of her why-do-I-have-to-put-up-with-these-peasants faces. "Common land. It's an old British tradition."

But because I'd already walked so far, and because she didn't trust me to find my way back from the long walk, we took the short walk — down her block, across the main street, and down to the river. It'd be pretty inaccurate to say that I took them, since they lurched and pulled the whole way (I didn't have to show them who was boss; they already knew). But once we got to the river path they calmed down and we had a really nice walk. There were a couple of small boats on the river and a heron, and there were other people with dogs or children just slouching along, enjoying the sunny day, and I almost felt right at home. You know, like I was strolling through Prospect Park.

When we got back to the house, Mrs. Payne ushered me into the living room. There was a tray on the coffee table that featured a flowery china pot and a plate of cookies.

"I thought we'd try that tea of yours."

I pointed to the large maroon book next to the tea tray. "What's that?"

She looked at it for a few seconds like she'd never seen it before. "Oh. Oh, that. I thought since you're interested in old things, you might like to see some of my photographs."

The funny thing was that I did. I never had any trouble picturing Sky when she was my age because she's never totally grown up. I mean, she still wears patchwork overalls and tie-dyed T-shirts and stuff like that. She hadn't grown up like Mrs. Payne. Mrs. Payne had obviously been a fully evolved adult for at least sixty years. I was really curious to see if she'd ever been young.

We went through two pots of tea.

The first part of the album was all pictures of London when there were hardly any cars and of Mrs. Payne's parents and brothers and sisters sitting in the garden or at the beach and stuff like that.

I was surprised about the brothers and sisters. "Caroline said she didn't have any family but you."

"She meant she doesn't have them now," said Mrs. Payne.

The second part was all during the war. (It was a lot longer war than Grandpa Gene led me to believe.) There were pictures of her brothers in uniforms and her eldest sister in a nurse's outfit and the other sister driving an ambulance.

"So what happened to them?" I persisted. "Where are they now?"

"They didn't make it." She put a finger on each picture in turn. "George went down over France. Robert was killed in the South Pacific. Beryl was blown up in the cinema. And Margaret married one of your lot and moved to California." She didn't exactly make it sound like marrying one of my lot and moving to California was an improvement on death. "Never saw her again."

Mrs. Payne turned to the last page of the album. "And this is our house after the bomb hit it."

That's what Jake always says about my half of the bedroom, that it looks like a bomb hit it. It doesn't. It just looks like I'm a slob. But the house Mrs. Payne grew up in did look like a bomb hit it. Maybe more than one. It was all rubble except that one of the fireplaces and the front door were still standing, like in some surreal dream.

"Jeez . . ." I stared hard at the photo. There was a woman's shoe and a doll on the road, as though someone had been running so fast from the planes that they'd dropped them. "It must've been horrible."

"We were lucky. Only the dog died that time."

The last picture in the album was of Mrs. Payne and a really young soldier. He had his arm around her and they were both smiling.

"Who's the dude?"

"You mean the young chap? That's Nigel Manders."

"Who was he? Was he your boyfriend?"

"You're a very nosy girl, aren't you?" For a second I thought she wasn't going to tell me, but then she said, "I suppose one could say he was my first love."

Oh, Great Earth Goddess! This woman had more hidden depths than the ocean.

"So what happened to him?"

She shut the album so fast I nearly got my finger caught. "He didn't make it either."

I said, "I'm sorry, Mrs. Payne. I didn't mean to upset you."

"I'm not upset." She heaved herself off the sofa to put the album away. "And I should think you could stop calling me Mrs. Payne. It sounds as if you're the maid."

"Well, what am I supposed to call you?"

She shoved the book onto the shelf. "Why, Nana Bea, of course."

I Have One of Those Days

Caroline's migraine liked her so much that it decided to hang out with her for nearly a week, and she stayed holed up in her room all that time like a bat in a cave.

Which pretty much left the rest of us to our own devices (as Sky would say).

Jake always says that if you don't expect things of people, then the chances are they'll never do them, and it looked like she was right. Robert's whole relationship with the kitchen before had been to eat in it or open a bottle of wine (he never had any trouble finding the corkscrew—that's for sure). But though he and I lived on takeout for a couple of days, we both got pretty sick of it and he finally decided to confront the kitchen like an ancient English warrior confronting an invading army. The invading army won the first couple of battles (I'd never thought of canned corn as a salad ingredient before and I'd also never realized that it's possible to bake a potato until it's raw), but eventually he not only learned how to slice bread; he discovered a talent for cooking (spaghetti and cheese omelet mainly, but it was a start). Robert said it actually helped him with the novel because ideas would come to him as he was opening the boxes and jars or beating the eggs.

And Nana Bea rose to the challenge, too. She was used to ordering Caroline around and not having to do anything but complain, but that didn't exactly work with me (I figured I was more like Jake than I thought). (I was even pretty sure she'd been reading the book I got her because she stopped griping about the fish and stuff and started saying that her back was feeling a bit better.) Every afternoon after I'd walked Drake and Raleigh she and I would have tea and go through another of her albums (she had about a hundred of them — you had to wonder when she'd ever found time to do anything else) or just discuss the past (she did the talking and I did the listening).

So things were going pretty tickety boo (if you weren't Caroline), in a quiet kind of way.

And then the rain started up again. Which (naturally) coincided with the first day Caroline felt strong enough to take charge of her mother again.

"Sod's Law," said Caroline. "If I were still laid up, the sun would be burning up the tarmac."

"Forget it," I advised. "You can't go sloshing around in this. You stay home. I'll walk Drake and Raleigh."

152

You couldn't say she put up much of a fight.

"Well, if you're certain . . ."

"Of course I am. I'm practically a professional dog walker by now."

(Of course, both Sod and Murphy could have told me that if you feel really confident about something, you're about to fall off a cliff.)

I blame the thunderstorm. Despite their names (which you'd at least think would give them a fondness for water), Drake and Raleigh don't like thunderstorms. Only I didn't know that until we were out of the house, me holding them with one hand and Caroline's umbrella with the other.

Nana Bea (who, you'll notice, didn't exactly mention the thing about English spaniels' sensitivity to sudden loud noises and flashes of light) waved to us from the front window. I waved back.

Which was pretty much the last thing I did of my own free will for the next half hour.

Just as I opened the gate, there was a crack of lightning that made it look as though the sky had been ripped open. It might as well have been the bolt of electricity that gives the monster life. Drake and Raleigh both left the ground like cartoon dogs, and then they lurched off in the opposite direction from the one we always took.

At the best of times (like when the sun was shining, I wasn't carrying an enormous umbrella with flowers all over it, and they weren't in Hitler and Karimov mode), I had my hands pretty full being lead dog, but at the worst of times (which this definitely was), I had less chance of making them do what I wanted then I had of getting the President to.

"Stop!" I shouted as thunder rumbled over Putney. It sounded like the Nazi bombers had returned. Drake and Raleigh started to run.

I pulled on their leashes. They picked up speed.

The wind (which seemed to be on their team) caught the umbrella and we sailed up the block, me shrieking commands and hanging on for all I was worth and them trying to outrun the storm. That didn't work either. There was another crack of lightning—gold, white, and purple—as we hit the corner. The dogs left the ground howling, and the umbrella and I more or less flew after them.

By the time the storm passed and they'd calmed down to their normal level of hysteria, I had no idea where we were. The block we were on looked pretty much like all the other blocks we'd been on, lined on either side by houses that looked pretty much like every other house we'd passed along the way.

Not that I was worried. Drake and Raleigh might be pretty psychotic, but they are dogs. You're always hearing those stories about dogs that walked for two years through blizzards and monsoons to find their way back home. It's part of their nature. And at first it seemed like that was what was happening. They dragged me on, stopping every few feet to examine a tire or a pole or try to get into somebody's garden, but they did it with determination. You know, like they knew where we were going.

But they didn't. We trudged on and on in what was by then a discouraged drizzle, but there was still no sign of Nana Bea's street. Every time we came to an intersection I'd stop and look in all directions. *Concentrate . . .* I told myself. *Look for landmarks . . . a car or a rosebush or a tricycle left on the sidewalk . . .* But all I saw was red-brick house after red-brick house, each with its tiny front garden and low brick wall. It was like staring at a flock of starlings trying to find the one whose life you saved when it was a baby and you called it Fred.

And then, way down at the end of an incredibly long street, I saw what looked like a small store. It was worth a chance.

I stared down at the dogs. "OK," I told them. "We're going down there to ask directions. And you two are going to wait outside and behave."

They looked like they understood. Raleigh even wagged his tail.

When we got to the end of the street, I tied them under the sign that said Aswani's Food Store, and went inside.

The only person in the store was a woman wearing a sari who was sitting behind the counter, reading a magazine.

She looked up and smiled in a helpful, friendly way.

I explained that I was visiting a friend and that I'd gotten lost and couldn't find my way back.

"And what road is it you are looking for?"

It was a reasonable question. It was the question I would have asked. Unfortunately, it wasn't a question I could answer. I couldn't remember. My mind was as blank as new snow. I used to know it. But after the first day, I knew where to turn automatically and it must have gone into a back file. And by then Drake and Raleigh and I had been up and down so many streets that all the names had kind of mushed together in my mind.

"Gamlen?" asked the woman. "Hotham? Bangalore?"

She somehow managed to make every name sound foreign and unfamiliar.

"Near the river?" she tried. "Away from the river?"

"Well, it's near the river, but it's away from the river, too."

"You are certain it is round here?"

I wasn't really sure of anything anymore. I felt as though I'd been sloshing through the rain for hours, which I pretty much had been. I could have been miles from where we started or just around the corner.

And then, as if the gods had finally decided to take pity on me, I heard someone outside calling Caroline's mother.

"Mrs. Payne! Mrs. Payne!"

A girl a couple of years older than I am burst into the store.

"Mrs. Payne, your do—" She stopped when she saw me.

"Tiki!" shouted the woman behind the counter. "Tiki? What is wrong?"

I already knew the answer to that question. "Oh, my God! The dogs!" I screamed, and ran past her so fast I nearly knocked her down.

Drake and Raleigh were loping down the street as fast as they could go.

I dropped the umbrella by the door and ran after them.

All I needed was to lose those dumb dogs. Nana Bea would make sure they brought back the fine old English tradition of hanging.

It wasn't until I spotted all this green and trees and other dogs dragging their owners through the rain up ahead that I realized where they were headed. They did know where they were going, after all. They were going to the common. By the time I caught up with them, they were chasing each other in circles on the soaking wet grass.

"What'd I tell you?" I shrieked. "Didn't I tell you to behave?"

The other dog walkers looked at me like I was nuts.

Drake and Raleigh, dedicated to doing whatever you didn't think they were going to, came bouncing over as if they'd been looking for me everywhere, and hurled themselves against me. So now we all looked like we'd been rolling in mud.

I was definitely having one of those days. You know, the kind that take all the joy and passion out of life. The kind that make you feel you'd be better off being a pebble or a three-toed sloth than a person. I think it was that and the fact that I was so relieved to see Drake and Raleigh that all of a sudden self-pity rolled over me like a tsunami. Bachman was right. I should never have left Brooklyn. I really liked Caroline, Robert, and Nana Bea, but that didn't make up for the fact that I was pretty lonely and bored. I started to cry.

"You dropped your umbrella."

It was the girl from the store. She was holding Caroline's umbrella over my head. "I came in the van. Come on, I'll take you back to Mrs. Payne's."

I was too stunned to answer.

"I'm Tiki." She held out the hand that wasn't holding the umbrella. "You must be Mrs. Payne's Yank from the Wild West."

I took her hand. "I'm Cherokee."

Tiki laughed. "Well, what do you know. We're both Indians."

This Is the Kind of Thing
That Happens When You Don't
Stick to the Tour Bus

Tiki was in college, studying architecture and urban planning, but she was working in her parents' store for the summer. My gran would have loved her. (Bachman said he pretty much did love her because she wasn't a boy, so he didn't have to worry that I was never coming home.) Tiki wanted to design houses that were environmentally positive (solar energy and stuff like that). Besides the planet, the other thing she was into was London. In her free time she liked to ride around the city on her scooter.

"Greater London's enormous," said Tiki. "I want to see every bit, so I can piece it all together in my mind. You know, not just what's here now but the history and all."

She believed that the more you knew about the past, the better chance you had of getting the future right.

"And besides that, it means I'm just the person to show you the things you won't see in New York." Tiki's boyfriend was in France for the summer and her college pals all lived somewhere else, so she was happy to have someone to hang out with. She may have been the same age as the Czar, but Tiki didn't think I was just a kid; she thought I was a person.

Since Tiki was also the only one close to my age that did seem to think I was a person, I was happy as a pig with a backpack to eat, but I wasn't sure I could survive another tour. I felt they were like eating okra — you know, you should try it once, but you wouldn't actually want to make a habit of it. I told her I didn't really like the idea of tours. I'd never actually been on one that wasn't led by Robert, but you see them a lot in New York. Everybody piling off the bus and following the guide like a flock of sheep. *Look at this. . . . Look at that. . . . You'll want a picture of this. . . .* And anyway, though it was really nice of her to offer and everything, I'd already seen the Tower and the Houses of Parliament and the Roman wall and a lot of other things I couldn't actually remember, so I figured I'd pretty much covered all the major sights.

"Not those sights," said Tiki. "We're going where no tour has gone before."

So when she wasn't working, Tiki would pick me up on her scooter and we'd hit the clogged and polluted roads of the city.

It was like taking someone on a tour of New York and going to Brooklyn, Queens, and Staten Island and leaving out the Statue of Liberty and the Empire State Building. North, south, east, west, Tiki's trusty scooter took us all over. We went to places like Clerkenwell Green, where the protest march that ended in Bloody Sunday started (I took a picture for Sky), and Cable Street, where the people in the neighborhood stopped the Fascists from marching in the 1930s (I took a picture for Grandpa Gene so he could get a clearer idea of exactly how long the war really was). We went past about a thousand houses where someone famous used to live, and about ten thousand where nobody famous ever lived. We went past these old cabbies' shelters (that were started so the drivers wouldn't all disappear into pubs in bad weather and get drunk). We went to this amazing roof garden on top of what used to be a department store; it has a stream and bridges and a lake and a pair of flamingoes. We went to this really old burial ground where William Blake and Daniel Defoe are buried (I took a picture for Jake) and this excellent cemetery where Karl Marx is buried (another picture for Sky). We drove down the road where Buckingham Palace is, but not so I could see the palace—so I could see the nose stuck to the side of Admiralty Arch. We saw the narrowest building and a really old pub where boxing started. We went to Petticoat Lane and Brick Lane to see the markets and eat bagels. We went to Tiki's

161

Aswanis, the Scolfields, and the Jemisons—and Nana Bea, of course." She looked up from the guest list she'd just written. "Is there anyone else you can think of?"

I said, "The Jemisons?"

Caroline must have heard some astonished surprise in my voice because she gave me a thoughtful look. "Daniel's parents."

I knew that. "I wasn't really asking who they were . . . I just thought—"

Caroline was still looking at me in a puzzled kind of way. Then her face lit up like someone had turned the light on. "Oh . . . you mean because of what happened with Sophie?"

"What happened with Sophie?"

I didn't mean that at all. I was thinking more of what happened with *me.*

Caroline glanced around the kitchen like she thought Sophie was about to walk through a wall and ask her what she thought she was doing talking about her. "I'm not meant to know anything about it, of course. All Sophie said was that she and Daniel broke up and that it was mutual and that they were still friends, but naturally Alison Scolfield told me as soon as she found out that Jocelyn was going out with him."

I decided to stick to born-yesterday mode. "Daniel used to go out with Sophie?"

"I don't think it was very serious. Sophie certainly didn't seem very upset by what happened. She and Jocelyn are still best mates."

Of course they were. That's why Sophie was in Brooklyn. And Jocelyn couldn't stop putting her down.

I managed a smile. "How nice."

"Besides," said Caroline, "I thought you and Daniel were friendly. He was ringing you every day for a while."

For six days. Jocelyn came back from her gran's at about the same time I'd run out of excuses for not hanging out with him.

"Oh, it's not that I don't like him or anything—" I loathed him. He was the slimeball from the Planet Creepton. "I—"

Was saved not by the bell but by our resident writer.

Robert stopped in the doorway as though he'd come into the wrong room. "What's the occasion, Cherry?" He looked worried, like he'd not only come into the wrong room but he was wearing his pajamas. "Are we having people to lunch?" It's the kind of thing he'd forget. "You're all dressed up."

I hadn't worn my lace skirt and my diamanté top since the day I arrived. They seemed a little fancy for dog walking or fooling around in the garden. "I'm going to Camden this afternoon."

"Thank God for that. I was afraid we had plans I didn't know about." He sat down with a sigh of relief. "But why on Earth would you want to go all the way up there?"

Caroline rolled her eyes. "For heaven's sake Robert, it's North London, not the North Pole."

"It's over the river." Like it was on the moon. It was like people who never go above 14th Street in Manhattan. He poured himself a cup of tea, then looked at me. "I'll repeat my question. Cherry, dear, why on Earth would you want to go all the way up there?"

"It's part of my unofficial tour of London."

"I thought we'd already had our tour of London." Robert looked a little offended. "I can't think I left much out."

"This is different. That was all the important tourist stuff, but this time I'm seeing all the things we don't have in New York that tourists don't see."

"Really? Like Karl Marx's grave?"

Been there, done that. "Exactly."

"Well, I'm impressed." He picked up his cup. "So how have you planned it? Do you have a guidebook?"

I bit into my toast. "I don't need a book. I've got Tiki."

"Tiki?" He looked at Caroline, then back at me. "And who or what is Tiki?"

"She's my friend. You know, the one I go out with all the time?"

Robert blinked. The man was so totally oblivious it was just as well he hardly left the house—he'd have a hard time finding his way back again.

"Mrs. Aswani's youngest daughter," said Caroline. "You know, from the shop round by Mum's."

"The Aswanis' daughter?"

Caroline huffed. "Oh, for heaven's sake, Robert, don't tell me you haven't seen her scooter out front."

"Well, how am I meant to know whose scooter it is? You could have ordered a pizza." He put his cup back down and turned to me. "So let me get this straight, Cherry. Are you saying that you didn't want to see Buckingham Palace, but you're going to see Camden?"

"That's right." I finished off my own cup of tea. "It's the Goth capital of the world."

Robert nodded really slowly. "Of course. How did I manage to overlook that?"

"You have a good time," said Caroline. "Don't forget, Nana Bea's coming for supper. Shall we say sevenish? That way you won't have to rush."

"That sounds great."

I figured I'd be back long before seven.

Which just shows how wrong you can be.

(Sod and Murphy strike again.)

Tiki and I spent hours wandering through the main market in Camden. I'd been to farmers' markets and street markets and craft fairs, but I'd never seen anything like it. This was the real deal. If there was a place like this anywhere in New York (even Queens!), I'd never shop anywhere else. Incense, candles, Celtic totems, silver earrings, Day of the Dead stuff, funky clothes, vintage gear, serious Goth gear, futuristic gear, and outrageous shoes . . . it was better than a dream come true because it's not something I would have been able to imagine till I saw it. I'd never have to make myself another skirt or cut up another pair of socks to wear as gauntlets again. There was even a part where they sold so many different kinds of food from all over the world that I wasn't sure what country we were in. After I'd pretty much spent my life's savings, we headed up the high street.

"Oh, wow! Look at that, Tiki. Jake would go nuts for this stuff."

Most of the shops had enormous 3-D signs out front—shoes, jackets, a giant chair, dice, and one even had Elvis. We definitely had nothing like this in Brooklyn.

"Didn't I tell you that you'd like Camden?"

"I do," I said. "I truly do."

There were about a million shoe stores with the most outrageous stuff. I bet this was where Mr. Wottle came to buy his daughter's killer boots.

There were tons of regular people milling around, but there were also so many really serious punks, hippies, and decked-out Goths that it looked like a film set (*The Addams Family* meets the Clash during the Summer of Love).

"Come on," said Tiki. "I've been saving the best for last."

The best was a real Goth pub where we could sit outside and eat potato chips and have a soda.

Only (as I've discovered often happens in life) we never made it to the pub.

We'd battled our way through the crowds to the road where we were supposed to turn left, when I saw the first sight I *really* never expected to see.

Just ahead of us, near the subway station, were two guys and a girl with signs and petitions. They looked like they'd just come from an anti-globilization demonstration. The girl had bright red hair and was wearing a pink tutu over her combat pants, and the guys were wearing old jeans and Indian shirts and strings of beads around their necks. The fairer of the two guys was talking to two dudes who looked totally straight and normal (NY baseball caps and jeans and Nike T-shirts, that kind of thing) except that they each held a can of beer and looked pretty mad about something.

"Good God!" I grabbed Tiki's arm and pulled her to a stop. "It's the Czar!"

Assuming that I'd either lost my mind or was making some weird Brooklyn joke, Tiki laughed. "The what?"

"The Czar. You know. Xar. Caroline's son."

"Here?" She smiled in that way people do when they think you must be seeing things. "Caroline's son? What would he be doing *here*?"

It looked like he was starting the revolution. I pointed her in the right direction. "There! Look up there. The guy with the sign that says END THIRD WORLD DEBT. The one who's doing the talking. That's the Czar." He might not speak to his parents, but he had no trouble talking to strangers.

168

"*That's* the Czar? I didn't think he'd look like that."

"What do you mean, you didn't think he'd look like that?"

"I don't know . . . I reckon I thought he'd be taller . . . or wearing a crown."

"Come on." I pulled on her arm. "Let's go see what's going on."

Tiki shrugged. "OK. We're in no hurry."

Timing really is everything, isn't it? If the first creature to crawl out of the primal soup had been beaned by an asteroid as soon as it poked its head out of the water, the whole history of the planet might have been different. And if we'd come up the street ten minutes sooner or ten minutes later, our Sunday would probably have had a completely different ending.

But we weren't ten minutes later or ten minutes sooner. We reached the Czar and his friends just as one of the beer drinkers started shouting some all-purpose abuse about their personal hygiene, their sexual practices, and what they could do with their petitions.

There might have been a lot of hippies around, but this definitely wasn't the Summer of Love.

"Uh-oh . . ." said Tiki. "It looks like somebody's let the dogs out."

The girl was shouting back at them, but the Czar and the other guy stayed calm as the Dalai Lama.

The Czar smiled. "I think what you suggested would be a bit of a physical impossibility."

Mr. Straight and Normal took a step forward. "I'll show you what's a physical impossibility."

"It's scum like you lot what's ruining this country," said his buddy.

The Czar's friend stepped closer to him. "Why don't you just move on, mate?"

"Don't you talk to me like that." Mr. Straight and Normal jabbed him in the chest with his can. "I ain't your mate."

The Czar sighed. "Look, just move on, all right? Nobody wants any trouble."

He wasn't exactly right about that. Passersby had started slowing down and hovering, the way people do when they think someone's going to jump off a roof.

Lots of us don't perform well in front of a crowd. Crowds make us shy and self-conscious. We don't like to be seen behaving badly or acting like a total jerk. But to others of us, seeing a crowd gathering is like pulling the pin on a grenade.

Mr. Straight and Normal and his buddy belonged to that second group. They puffed themselves up like cats getting ready for a fight.

"You're the one who's causing the trouble," the second man snarled back. This time the Czar was jabbed so hard that he staggered backward.

The girl stepped between them. "Oi!" she screamed. "Push off, you yobs!"

Mr. Straight and Normal pushed her off and right into me.

That's when Tiki decided to get involved.

170

"Hang on." She touched Mr. Straight and Normal on the shoulder. "What sort of bloke treats a woman like that? You keep your hands off her."

The two beer drinkers turned around at the same time.

"And who's going to make me?" demanded Mr. Straight and Normal.

Beer Man Two said, "Bleedin' heck, that's all we need, a bloody Paki." The other scum that was ruining the country, obviously. "Why don't you go back where you came from?"

Thank God we were in the most civilized country in the world, a beacon of freedom and democracy for all the oppressed people of the earth.

"You mean Putney?" said Tiki.

Because the beer men were glaring at Tiki and because the girl in the tutu and I were next to Tiki, the Czar finally noticed me. "Oi," he said. "Don't I know you?"

You don't really want to get distracted when a couple of meatheads want to prove how much better they are than you by beating you up. You've got to keep your eye on the ball, as we say back in Brooklyn.

In the second that the Czar took his eye off the ball to wonder where he'd seen me before, one of the upholders of the British Way of Life threw a real punch. Blood gushed out of the Czar's nose.

There wasn't any time to offer first aid. In about

half a second beer cans and signs and petitions and fists were flying all over the place.

In about sixty seconds, a cop had appeared and you could hear a siren wailing toward us.

The Czar and his friends made a run for it, but the Knights of the Beer Hall Table just kept ranting and kicking their signs around, and Tiki and I just stood there, not sure what to do next.

Not that there was much we could do.

"Looks like your mates've scarpered," said one of the cops.

"They're not our mates," said Tiki. "We were just walking by."

The first cop smiled in a really unfriendly way. "Of course you were."

"I'm not even English," I protested. "I'm a visitor to your shores."

"Well, welcome to Britain," said another cop.

The inside of a police car was another sight I hadn't planned on seeing.

(Lesson for Today: Don't make plans.)

The Perfect End
to a Perfect Day

I was a little worried that since I was an alien and everything, I might be returned to Putney in the back of a police car (possibly handcuffed). Nana Bea might think that was pretty cool, but I wasn't so sure about Caroline and Robert. I mean, what if the press was alerted? *Does Art imitate Life, or is it the other way around? Mystery writer Robert Pitt-Turnbull must have thought he was in one of his own novels yesterday when officers of the Met paid him a visit.* Not only would it scandalize the neighbors, but there was a strong possibility that it would give poor Caroline a migraine to make all others look like a complete absence of pain.

Everything got straightened out at the police station (another thing I hadn't exactly planned on seeing). I mean, you didn't have to be Sherlock Holmes to figure out that Tiki and I weren't exactly Public Enemies Numbers One and Two.

(Besides, we weren't the ones who were drunk and yelling at everybody!)

And the cops were really nice. They said I was seeing a London most visitors never saw.

"Right," I said. "Go to Big Ben, go to Hyde Park, go directly to jail."

Tiki said it was probably the London no one wanted to see.

"I certainly didn't want to see it," said Tiki. "Next time we'll try to leave out the aggressive racists."

I said it didn't matter because the same thing could have happened in the States. I told her how some guy on Long Island tried to run over a woman in the parking lot of a mall because she was a Muslim.

Anyway, what with one thing and another, it was almost seven by the time I got home.

By then I'd pretty much had enough surprises for one day, but I should have known that they weren't over yet.

I hadn't even put my key in the front door when it opened as if I'd said the magic words.

The Czar had finally found his way back home and had been waiting for me. He'd changed into a shirt that didn't have any blood stains on it and his nose hadn't swelled up or turned blue or anything, so unless you'd been with him, you'd never know that he hadn't spent the afternoon reading a book.

"Cherry," he said. "I—"

I was way past being polite to *him*. "It's

Cherokee, remember? Like the Indians." And this time they were ready for war.

That was as far as we got because Robert popped out of the kitchen just then like a cuckoo out of a clock. "We were beginning to get a bit worried." He had a knife in one hand and a carrot in the other.

Caroline was right behind him. She was wearing oven mitts. "Oh, there you are. I was worried you might have had an accident."

Right behind her was Nana Bea. "Didn't I tell you she was fine? She was just having a good time, weren't you, Cherry?"

"Yeah." I shut the door. I had a pretty good idea what the Czar wanted to say to me (keep your trap shut), but he was going to have to wait. I wanted him to suffer. "It was brilliant."

"Well, you'll have to tell us all about it over supper," said Nana Bea.

Robert waved the carrot at the Czar. "The prodigal son has shown up to dine on the fatted nut roast with us!"

Caroline beamed. "Isn't this nice? We're finally going to have a real family meal."

Behind me, I heard the Czar groan.

A family meal in Brooklyn usually means that everybody's talking at once, but in Putney we all took turns.

Nana Bea got the floor first. She told us about her adventures taking Drake and Raleigh for a walk around the block that afternoon.

The Czar yawned.

"Your back must be feeling much better," said Robert.

She said a bit.

Last week she'd gone with me, Drake, and Raleigh on our walks, and had even made it down to the Aswanis' twice on her own.

I said I bet it was that book that had done the trick.

"Book?" Nana Bea blinked as though she was trying to remember what book I meant. "Oh, the book. Oh, no, no, I don't think it could be that. I don't even know where I put it."

It's sad to see an old lady lie.

"I thought I saw it in your living room," I said. "On the shelf under the coffee table."

"And what about you, Caroline?" asked Nana Bea. "What have you been doing with all your free time?"

When she wasn't working in the garden, she was working in the garden shed. Apparently painting helped keep the migraine away.

Caroline did her Mona Lisa smile. "Oh, this and that . . ."

Robert's day had been hell. Apparently it was easier to dig to the center of the earth with a spoon than finish chapter twelve.

"You were in here listening to the radio and chopping nuts most of the afternoon," said Caroline.

"It doesn't mean I wasn't working," answered Robert. "Besides, somebody had to do it."

Then it was my turn at bat. I told them about the market, and the shops, and all the different people and stuff like that. I said we'd even gone to this brilliant Goth pub. I said that was why I was late getting back, because we'd gotten so involved in just watching everyone and stuff that we'd lost track of the time.

And all the time I was talking, the Czar watched me like I was the cat and he was the mouse. He didn't say anything. But I could hear him thinking: *Don't mention cops. . . . Don't mention protests. . . . Don't mention fistfights. . . . Don't mention racial slurs. . . . Whatever you do, don't mention me.* I was almost tempted to say something about what had happened just to see what he'd do. Leap across the table and drag me out of the room? Pretend he was having some sort of fit? Prove that he really was going to have a great future in politics by lying through his teeth?

"So what about you, Xar?" asked Robert when I was done. "What did you get up to today?"

I gave the Czar my full, wide-eyed attention.

"Same old same old," said the Czar. "Hung out with my mates."

Which pretty much made him the only person in the kitchen who was strictly sticking to the truth.

I lit the candles and incense on my altar and put on my Buddhist chants CD. Unlike Jake, there was no way Caroline would disturb me if she thought I was meditating. She's too seriously polite.

177

When I was done with all that, I turned off the light and sat down on the bed. "Right," I said. "Start talking."

The Czar was sitting at the desk. He leaned forward. "Look," he said, "I didn't mean to do a runner like that and drop you and your friend in it. But if I got nicked, my parents would find out."

"So what? You're an activist, not a serial killer." I sat up straight the way Nana Bea did when she was about to explain how you were wrong about something. "And besides, I thought you didn't even live here anymore. I thought you were *off*."

He might not have inherited his mother's smile, but he'd gotten her sigh down pat. "You don't understand."

And that was what? *My* fault?

"Of course I don't understand. That's why you're supposed to be talking to me, remember?"

"I haven't precisely moved out. I was only taking a break from them. They wouldn't understand either."

"They wouldn't understand that you're concerned about the world?"

He was starting to sound like something being deflated.

"Surely my mother told you about their plans for me?"

"You mean going to Oxford and being a lawyer and maybe a politician?"

From the expression on his face, you'd think he'd just realized that the smell he hadn't been able

178

to identify was decomposing flesh. "Those are the plans."

"You mean you don't want to do any of that?"

He didn't know. He wasn't sure. He had his doubts. He needed time to think.

"What I want to do is go back to India. Or maybe to South America. Do volunteer work. Find out what I'm really interested in."

Caroline had been right. He had picked up something while he was away.

I didn't see what the big deal was. So he'd changed his mind. I've been known to change my mind in the middle of a sentence.

"They have expectations," said the Czar.

I didn't really get the expectation thing either. Jake's expectations tend to be things like not becoming a corporate lawyer or a drug addict.

"So?"

"My dad always wished he'd gone into law, like his father. And my mother's family—" It was the first time his smile had been even in the neighborhood of humor. "Well, you've met my grandmother—she thinks her family put the Great in Britain." He put on a face that looked remarkably like Nana Bea telling you that she's drunk Earl Grey tea since she was in the womb. "Our family survived the Peasants' Revolt, you know."

"So that means they'll be able to survive this without any trouble." I said that if his dad had wanted to be a lawyer, then he should've done it, not expect somebody else to do it for him.

179

"You don't understand. I can't bear to disappoint them. The guilt would drive me mad."

I pointed out that he was disappointing them now, sneaking around like an enemy agent.

"Yeah . . . Well . . ." He'd been fiddling with the computer mouse, but now he shoved it aside and started looking for dust mites in the carpet. "There is something else. . . ."

And, oh, how I wondered what that could be, right?

When he didn't say anything for a couple of minutes, I said, "And this something else is what—animal, vegetable, or mineral?"

"Well, I sort of met someone in India, didn't I?" He raised his head. "You know, that's what got me interested in politics and all. Made me see things differently."

"And?"

"Well, it's sort of complicated, isn't it?"

"How can I know that when you won't tell me what it is?"

Apparently this question required him to really concentrate on counting the dust mites in the carpet before it could be answered.

"Oh, for Pete's sake." Patience may be a virtue, but it's not one of mine. "I've seen you together. I know all about it."

He looked confused, like I'd made him lose count. "You do?"

"Of course. I've seen you together a bunch of times." Three times seemed pretty conclusive to me.

"Who are we talking about here?"

Oh, Great Earth Goddess, please give me the strength to deal with really difficult people.

"That girl with the bright red hair."

"Oh, Celeste. I don't think you understand—"

"Of course I understand. She's from a different class right?" I saw that movie *Gosford Park*; I knew all about the class system. "And because of her politics and the hair and the tutu and everything." (Everything being her tendency to yell at big men who obviously had no policy against hitting women.) "You don't think your parents will like her."

"Well, you're right there. They wouldn't like her anymore than they'd like . . ."

"But that's where you're wrong." I was certain as a missionary. "How do you know they won't like her? They haven't met her."

"Trust me. I know my parents. They wouldn't like her or—"

"Well, I don't think they really liked me at first, but now they do."

"Right," he said, "but you're going home."

"Thanks."

"You know what I mean."

"I still think you should give them the benefit of the doubt. Why don't you just introduce them to Celeste?"

"Hang on. Celeste is—"

"No, listen to me. Once they get to know her—"

"First of all, they wouldn't get to know her,

181

would they? They'd dislike her on sight. And if they *did* get to know her, they'd really dislike her." He looked like he was thinking of banging his head on the desk. "And Celeste's no different, really. Forget about the Peasants' Revolt. She's all set to wage the French Revolution again — only this time in Britain."

Humans really do make things complicated, don't they?

But since I was raised by people who were always breaking down in deserts and on remote mountaintops, I'm resourceful.

"Well how about this? What if Caroline and Robert meet Celeste casually? You know, not actually knowing who she is?"

"You mean we just happen to bump into them on the street?"

"I was thinking more of the garden."

"In the garden?"

"At the barbecue."

"What barbecue?"

He was definitely related to Robert.

"My good-bye barbecue. Tons of people are going to be there. You could invite all your other friends, too. You know, confuse them."

For the first time he looked at me as though I might be speaking English. "You mean they wouldn't see the tree for the forest?"

"Exactly."

I couldn't have put it better myself.

If There's One Thing You Can Always Depend on, It's the English Weather

When I told Caroline that the Czar wanted to invite some of his friends to the barbecue she went into what-language-are-we-speaking-now mode.

"Friends?" said Caroline. "Xar wants to invite his friends? *Here?*"

"Not all of them," I assured her. "Just a few."

Caroline shook her head. "But why on Earth would he want to do that?"

"Because he wants you to meet them."

"Because he wants us to meet them." She smiled bravely, like she was coming down this dark alley at three in the morning and she knew what was going to be waiting for her at the end. "I see." Caroline sighed. "Oh, Lord." She stared down at her tea. "I do hope this doesn't mean he wants to marry her."

I hadn't expected her to unravel my complex and supremely clever scheme so quickly.

"Oh, I don't think it's anything like that," I said quickly. "He just thought it's time you—"

"Met his friends," finished Caroline. "I wasn't born yesterday, you know. I know what that means." She lifted her cup as though it was filled with solid gold. "He's bringing the girl."

All Robert wanted to know was if they ate meat or not. They didn't.

"God help us," said Robert. "We're being swamped by veggies. We'll have to get another grill."

"His friends?" said Nana Bea. "Well, I'd say it's about time, don't you?"

It didn't look like my idea of hiding the tree in the forest was going to work exactly the way I'd thought. Nana Bea said it was like the elephant in the room. Everybody knew it was there, but no one was going to mention it, especially not to the Czar. They acted like all they were nervous about was if there'd be enough pasta salad and what the weather would be like.

The weather was perfect.

Caroline stared out the kitchen window like there was a unicorn chomping on her roses. "I can't believe it. There isn't a cloud in the sky."

"What did I tell you?" Robert lifted an apron from the box he'd just taken from the closet under the stairs and held it up. It was red and said B B KING in large white letters on the front. "It's not going to rain on barbecue day. Not this time."

The Czar and I put tables and chairs around the garden while Nana Bea supervised and Drake and Raleigh got under everybody's feet.

Robert set up the two barbecues with a table between them.

Caroline strung colored lights all around the garden.

"Who's going to see them?" asked Robert. "It's daylight."

"Well, you never know . . ." Caroline shrugged. "It might go on till late."

"It doesn't get dark till gone ten," Robert squawked. "You don't expect them to stay till gone *ten*, do you?"

"Well, it depends whether or not they're having a good time, doesn't it?" said Caroline.

The Czar's friends arrived first. There were five of them. Three of them had dreads and all of them were pierced. Celeste was wearing a green tutu today and a T-shirt that said ROB THE RICH. She was the only one who dressed up.

"Good God," muttered Robert as they slouched down the hallway. "They look like they just came from an antiglobalization demonstration."

"I wonder which one it is," murmured Caroline.

The Czar introduced them. Carlos, Rosen, Evelina, Jack, Celeste.

Carlos said, "Pleased to meet you."

Rosen said, "Cheers."

Evelina thanked Caroline and Robert for inviting her.

Jack was the one I'd seen at Parliament Square and in Camden. He said it was a pleasure to meet us all.

185

Celeste had never met a writer or a painter before.

"My parents' friends tend to be more realistic," said Celeste. She turned to Robert. "Not to be bad or anything, but how can you write novels when the world's going to hell?"

Robert smiled like he'd probably heard this question before (and probably from his son). "Just because a book's a work of fiction doesn't mean it isn't true. Which is more than can be said about a lot of nonfiction."

"Well, I'll say one thing . . ." Celeste was looking around the dining room like she was planning to steal the silver. "The book business must be better than I thought. Maybe I should give up trying to save the world and write a novel."

"Come on." The Czar took her by the elbow. "Let's go in the garden."

"I don't really *get* gardens," muttered Celeste as he dragged her away. "I mean, first you destroy the natural landscape and then you spend all your spare time trying to re-create it but without any of the inconvenient things like insects and animals."

"Well . . ." said Robert.

Caroline sighed.

"She's got her share of opinions, that one," said Nana Bea.

(Proving that old saying of Sky's: It takes one to know one.)

Jack asked Robert if he needed any help.

"To tell you the truth," said Robert as they led

186

the way through the French doors. "I could use a veggie grill chef."

"Brilliant," said Jack. "I've been looking forward to having a chance to talk to you. I understand you're something of an expert on the Victorians."

Next to turn up were the Aswanis. Mrs. Aswani was truly resplendent in a sari that was as bright and glittery as a Christmas tree.

"Cool," said Tiki, taking in the Czar's friends. "They've moved the revolution to the Pitt-Turnbulls' backyard. That's much more convenient. Plus they're serving drinks and food."

The Scolfields and the Jemisons arrived at the same time. The mothers were both in floaty, flowery summer dresses and the fathers and Daniel were in slacks and short-sleeved shirts, but Jocelyn looked like she'd just stepped out of a Gap ad for summer fun.

Jocelyn nodded to the rebel army that had gathered around a bowl of chips and dip. "Where did that lot come from?"

I said they were Xar's friends.

"Ugh. They look like anarchists." Jocelyn grimaced. "And he used to be so normal."

"The one in the skirt would be pretty if her hair was a normal color," said Daniel.

Jocelyn pretended to laugh, but her eyes were glaring. "Oh, puh-lease . . ."

It started off really well.

The Aswanis and Nana Bea got into a heavy

discussion about back pain. Mr. Aswani was a fellow sufferer.

"I've got a very good book that helped me," said Nana Bea. "You can borrow it if you'd like."

The Pitt-Turnbulls' friends all swarmed around together, talking gardens.

Tiki, Rosen, Carlos, and Evelina found they had a common interest in solar energy.

Jack and Robert huddled over the grills together, talking like they had to use up every word in their heads in the next hour or be turned into weevils.

And then it started to rain.

Caroline sighed. "It looks like it's Plan B."

I figured Plan B was cook in the kitchen.

"Nonsense," said Robert. "Humans didn't get where they are today by not being adaptable. Caroline, fetch the umbrellas."

Apparently this had also happened before because Robert had two clamp-on umbrellas that he attached to bamboo poles stuck into pots on either side of the barbecues to keep the coals from going out (which was pretty ingenious for a man who'd just learned how to slice bread).

The rest of us (except for Jocelyn and Daniel, who had disappeared into the house as soon as they'd said hello to everybody) beat a hasty retreat inside.

Out in the garden we all sort of milled around, but there wasn't enough room to mill around in the dining room. We kind of broke off into two groups

—the Pitt-Turnbulls' friends around the table near the French doors, where the wine was, and Nana Bea, the Aswanis, and the Czar's pals more in the middle of the room. Tiki, Carlos, and Evelina stopped talking about solar power and started talking about water. The Czar and the Aswanis got into a conversation about India. Celeste and Nana Bea were swapping protest stories. I was just thinking of going to see if Caroline needed any help in the kitchen when Jocelyn and Daniel finally decided to join the merrymakers. They both looked rumpled.

Jocelyn bore down on me like a heat-seeking missile.

"There you are!" she called. "I was wondering where you'd got to."

"That's funny," I said. "I was wondering the same thing about you."

"I just wanted to tell you how sorry I am that I never rang you when I got back from my grandmother's. I just didn't have a chance."

The girl was kindness and consideration given human form.

"That's OK," I said. "I was pretty busy, too."

She didn't ask.

Jocelyn launched into a detailed account of everything she and Daniel had been doing that had kept her so busy. It might have gone on for hours, but somewhere around ". . . and then we took a picnic to Kew—have you been to Kew?—oh, you really should go . . ." Jocelyn got distracted by something behind me. She kept talking, but it was like the voice you get when you call the movie theater to find out what time the shows are. Her eyes were staring over my shoulder like she was trying to move the furniture through telepathy.

I glanced around.

Nana Bea had joined Tiki, Evelina, Rosen, and Carlos. Daniel was talking to Celeste. He was standing almost on top of her (which, to be fair, was pretty hard not to do), with an expression on his face that I figured was supposed to be serious and intent but that looked more like constipation. Celeste was carrying the burden of the conversation, with Daniel nodding wisely every sentence or two.

I turned back to Jocelyn. "Isn't that nice?" I grinned. "Daniel's made a friend."

She put a smile as bright as a surgical knife on her face and walked past me. I automatically followed her.

"There you are." All warm and bubbly, she came up beside Daniel and slipped her arm around his waist. "I've been looking for you everywhere." (No one was going to criticize Jocelyn for being too original.) She leaned her head against his shoulder. "And you are?" The warmth and bubble died out when she spoke to Celeste. "I don't think we've been introduced."

Celeste looked at Jocelyn for a full nanosecond. "Celeste." She looked back to Daniel. "Anyway, as I was saying, it's no good just giving people aid. You have to change the system that keeps them—"

Jocelyn cut her off again. "You know, I've always loved that picture." She was gazing up at the portrait of Mr. Bean as though it was the ceiling of the Sistine Chapel. "Don't you think it's just brilliant?"

"Yeah, yeah, it's good," Daniel mumbled.

Celeste spoke clearly, distinctly, and loudly. "Personally, I don't really get that sort of thing. I mean, pictures of pets . . . they're nice and all, but tens of thousands of children die every day of poverty. Don't you think it seems a bit frivolous to paint pictures of cats?"

"Well . . . umm . . ." Daniel mumbled.

"No, I don't," answered Jocelyn. "Art is what separates man from the beasts."

"What crap," snapped Celeste. "What separates man from the beasts is a death wish."

"A death wish?" Jocelyn coughed out a few pained laughs. "Oh, puh-lease. I know all about global warming and the starving millions in the Third World and all that, but we have a civilization our great-grandparents couldn't even have imagined."

"Oh, really?" Arguing with policemen and politicians all the time had paid off for Celeste; she had scorn down pat. "And just what is it you do with all this brilliant civilization? Go shopping?"

Since this seemed to be pretty much what Jocelyn did do with all this brilliant civilization, she answered with an attack. "And what do you do? Stand in the road, chanting?"

191

Celeste sneered. "Sometimes. I sure as hell do more than people like you with your shallow, self-centered consumerist existence."

"At least I contribute to the economy." Jocelyn had a pretty good sneer too. "And perhaps if you did a little consuming now and then, you wouldn't look like a clown."

Celeste finally worked out how to smile. "Looking like a clown is a sight better than looking like a walking Gap ad."

I figured it was time to stop this conversation since it was starting to look about as attractive as an open wound.

"Hey, Jocelyn." I put a hand on her shoulder. "I think lunch is almost ready. You want to see if Caroline needs some help in the kitchen?"

Jocelyn pulled away from my touch. "You help her."

Celeste went into mock-innocent mode. "What's the matter? Not used to doing any work?"

"*Me*? Look who's talking. People like you don't want to work and make a good life for themselves. You just want everything handed to you."

To be fair to Celeste, she stayed cool and calm for a change. "It looks to me like you're the one who's had everything handed to her."

Jocelyn, however, had zipped past cool and calm and was going straight into blind fury.

"And it looks to me like you're someone who takes everything she can get her grubby paws on."

"Jocelyn," I said, "I think maybe you should chill

out a little. You're getting way overheated here. Celeste didn't do anything to you. She just—"

"She didn't do anything to me?" Jocelyn swung around so fast I thought I was going to bite her nose. "She's only been making moves on my boyfriend since we got here."

Celeste making moves on Daniel was pretty much the equivalent of Subcomandante Marcos trying to get it on with Britney Spears, but I managed not to laugh out loud.

"Jocelyn, I really don't think that—"

"Well, pardon me, but I think I know what I've seen with my own two eyes."

"Do you?" I blame the confined space for what I said next. Stuffing a bunch of people into a small room is like sticking a bunch of rats in a cage. It's unnatural and stressful. "Well, what I've seen with my own two eyes is *your boyfriend* making moves on every breathing female within a ten-mile radius."

"I think I'll go and see what's happening in the garden," said Daniel, but since Jocelyn was still wrapped around him like a snake, he didn't actually go anywhere.

Jocelyn was definitely the exception to the rule that girls look pretty when they're angry. "I should've known you'd stick up for the scum of the earth. Daniel does not—"

"He made a move on you when he was going out with Sophie."

It was a guess, but it was a pretty good one.

"It wasn't like—"

193

"He made a move on me that time we went shopping."

I think Daniel groaned, but it was hard to tell because of the shriek made by Jocelyn.

Which was quickly followed by her bursting into tears and running from the room.

"Jocelyn!" shouted Daniel, and he ran after her.

"Why can't you ever just let anything go?" the Czar shouted at Celeste. "You never know when to stop."

"And you never know when to start," Celeste screamed back. "I knew it was a mistake coming here!" And she followed Jocelyn and Daniel a whole lot faster than night follows day.

"Oh, dear." Caroline's head had appeared at the serving hatch. "Is something wrong?"

The front door banged shut.

Jocelyn's mother put down her drink. "I'm so sorry, Caroline, but I'm afraid Jocelyn's a bit upset. We've had a wonderful time, but I really think we should go."

"Oh, but you can't leave now." Caroline looked like she might hurl herself over the bowls of salad she'd put on the ledge of the hatch to stop the Scolfields from leaving. "You haven't had your lunch."

Carlos, Rosen, and Evelina all looked at one another.

"Maybe we should cut, too," said Carlos.

Evelina and Rosen were already shifting toward the door.

Mrs. Jemison put down her glass. "I think we'd better be going, too. It really is getting late."

"Please." Caroline came charging into the dining room. "I'm certain that whatever's happened can be easily sorted. Please stay. We're almost ready to eat."

But Mrs. Scolfield and Mrs. Jemison were already only a few steps behind the forces of the revolution.

"We must do this again before the summer's out, Caroline." Mr. Scolfield took his car keys from his pocket. "Perhaps when it isn't raining."

"But—" Caroline bleated as the Jemisons and the Scolfields filed out around her. "But we've made all this food—"

She was still standing there when the French doors burst open and Robert and Jack stepped in with slightly wet platters of burgers.

"Good God!" Robert looked around the room. "Have we been out there that long? Has everyone gone home?"

Jack turned to the Czar. "What happened?"

The Czar made a what-do-you-think kind of face. "Celeste went off on one."

"And Jocelyn," I added. "Jocelyn went off on one first."

Nana Bea shook her head. "Well, I can't say I think much of your choice in women, Alexander. I can't imagine why you'd be interested in someone so bossy."

The Czar gave her a puzzled smile. "What are you on about?"

"Celeste, of course," snapped Nana Bea. "Never mind this 'opposites attract' nonsense. You'd be much better off with someone more like you."

"Celeste?" The Czar stopped smiling. "Celeste's not my girlfriend."

"She isn't?" That wasn't the impression he gave *me*.

"But we thought that was why you invited your friends today. So we could meet her." Caroline was looking around the room like there might be a girl hidden behind a chair. Who is it if it's not Celeste?"

Jack smiled at everyone over the veggie burgers. "I think that would be me," said Jack.

"Well, thank God for that," said Robert.

The Final Episode, in Which We Bid a Fond Farewell to the People and Places of Putney

Caroline stopped at the front door. "Now are you sure you've got everything?" she asked me. "Passport? Ticket?"

Even though I'd checked that I had them, her asking me again made me think maybe I hadn't, so I checked again.

"Got 'em."

"And all your bits and bobs?"

"I think so." I knew I had all the really important things—the Scottie dog pin that used to belong to Nana Bea's sister, the signed copy of one of Robert's mysteries, the portrait of me and Raleigh and Drake that Caroline painted, and a photo of me, the Czar, Jack, and Tiki outside the Goth pub in Camden.

"For God's sake, Caroline," shouted Robert from beside the car. "If she forgot anything, we'll post it to her. But if we don't get a move on, we'll be posting *her*."

"You know we're all going to miss you, don't you?" said Caroline as we finally climbed into the car. "What with one thing and another, it's been quite a summer."

"You can say that again," said Robert. "In six short weeks Cherry's managed to totally disrupt our lives. She's got me cooking, she's got the Red Queen doing exercises, she's got you painting, and—as if that wasn't enough—she's turned our son into a homosexual. I'd say that's not bad going for only six weeks. God knows what would happen if she'd stayed any longer."

You had to admire the way they'd all come along, really.

"There's something I have to tell you," I said. It had been bothering me practically since I got there, but somehow I could never bring myself to correct them. "I've felt really bad about it. I mean, I know I should've told you before—"

Robert pulled into the road. "Good God! What else have you done?"

"It's not something I did. It's just—"

Caroline turned around to look at me. "For heaven's sake, Cherry, what is it?"

"That's it." I'd been debating confessing for the last two days. But it seemed wrong not to tell them. "My name isn't Cherry. It's Cherokee."

"Oh, we know that." Caroline laughed. "I just thought Cherry was so much easier."

"And it doesn't sound like a car," said Robert.

. . . And Say Hello Again to Good Old Brooklyn

After Jake and the kids went to bed, Bachman, Bruce Lee, and I went and sat on the front stoop. Even though it was dark, it was still so hot that it felt like the Great Earth Goddess had cranked up the heat and forgotten about it and gone out. It was just like always. You'd think I'd never been away. Well, almost.

Usually you couldn't shut Bachman up, but tonight he didn't seem to have anything to say. He just sat there, staring over at the Scutaris'.

"So," I said. "It sounds like you had a pretty good summer after all."

"Yeah." He nodded at the Scutaris' porch. "Yeah, I did."

"I mean, Sophie wasn't so bad, right?"

"Yeah, she was OK. Once she stopped running away from me and chilled out. She almost reminded me of you."

I could have kicked him. What is it with guys? You can't turn your back on them. One minute they're all warped out of shape because you're going away, and the next they're having this mega-great time without you. "Trust me," I said. "She's nothing like me. I've seen her room."

He looked at me out of the corner of his eye. "Sounds like you had a good time, too."

I said that it was brilliant. I was going to add that he would have loved it (especially all the run-ins with the law) but I decided not to. I didn't want him to think that I would have liked him to be with me. Instead I said, "So, you think you'll ever see the Pitt-Turnbull again?"

"Maybe." Bachman shrugged. "I was thinking maybe on the way back from seeing Europe."

From seeing Europe? Had aliens taken over his body while I was gone? "*You?* You're going to see Europe?"

He shrugged again. "I was thinking—you know, after graduation. It doesn't sound as bad as I thought."

"I suppose that's all because of Sophie." I was trying not to sound shrill or anything, but I wasn't sure I was succeeding.

"Sophie?" He gave me one of his will-I-ever-understand-you looks. "What's Sophie got to do with it? It's because of you. You got me interested."

You have only yourself to blame, is what Sky would have said. Why didn't I ever listen to her?

Our shoulders had been sort of touching, but I straightened up and moved a little away.

"Now what?" Bachman looked over at me. "All of a sudden you're mad at me?"

"I'm not mad at you."

"You're acting like you're mad at me."

I bent down to pet Bruce Lee. He growled.

"You see?" said Bachman. "Even he knows." This time he bent down to pet Bruce Lee. He wagged his tail. "What's the matter? You don't want to go to Europe?"

"Me?"

"Well, yeah, you. You don't think I'd go without you, do you?"

"You wouldn't?"

"Of course not." He scratched Bruce Lee behind the ears. "I missed you."

I shuffled over so our shoulders were touching again. "Really?"

"Yeah, really."

I took his hand from Bruce Lee and held it in mine. "I missed you, too."